Suzanne was drowning in pleasure

She had the cold counter at her back and a hard, warm Ryan at her front and she'd never felt so hot in her life. The shadows lent to the intimacy, which threatened to overwhelm her.

"This is just what we said, right? No more, no less," she said on a gasping breath.

"Sex." Ryan's deep voice sent another thrill through her.

"*Just* sex. And when we're done…"

"We're done," he finished. Was she imagining things or did he sound skeptical, as though he didn't believe what he'd just said?

"Right. Itch scratched." She was panting now, and so was he.

"Right."

For the longest moment he just looked at her, her dark and beautiful man. Then he groaned, pulled her even closer and she melted against him. His mouth was so firm, and so deliciously demanding, she couldn't help but sink into the mindlessness of it, needing the mindlessness of it. He had a wonderful mouth, a make-her-forget-everything mouth, and he knew just what to do with it to make her wild.

And she intended on getting very, *very* wild….

Dear Reader,

I'm so excited about this book, as it's the first in my
three-book Temptation miniseries SOUTH VILLAGE
SINGLES. I loved the idea of writing a series about three
friends who make a vow of singlehood. And I started
thinking about the sexy, irresistible men who could tempt
them to break that vow. Just what kind of man would it
take to break a vow between friends—especially since
we're talking about strong, independent women! Guess
you'll have to read on to find out.

I hope you enjoy reading Suzanne's story—and have
fun with her as she tries so hard to resist the very
charming Ryan. Be sure to catch Nicole's story in
Tangling With Ty available in February, and Taylor's
story, *Messing With Mac,* available in March, as all three
of them fall hard and fast in the most unexpected ways....

Happy reading,

Jill Shalvis

P.S. I love to hear from readers! You can reach me
through my Web site www.jillshalvis.com or by writing
me at P.O. Box 3945, Truckee, CA 96160-3945.

Books by Jill Shalvis

HARLEQUIN TEMPTATION
742—WHO'S THE BOSS?
771—THE BACHELOR'S BED
804—OUT OF THE BLUE
822—CHANCE ENCOUNTER
845—AFTERSHOCK
861—A PRINCE OF A GUY
878—HER PERFECT STRANGER
885—FOR THE LOVE OF NICK

HARLEQUIN DUETS
28—NEW AND...IMPROVED?
42—KISS ME, KATIE!
HUG ME, HOLLY!
57—BLIND DATE DISASTERS
EAT YOUR HEART OUT
85—A ROYAL MESS
HER KNIGHT TO REMEMBER

HARLEQUIN BLAZE
63—NAUGHTY BUT NICE

Jill Shalvis
Roughing It With Ryan

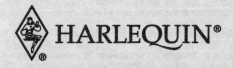

HARLEQUIN®

TORONTO • NEW YORK • LONDON
AMSTERDAM • PARIS • SYDNEY • HAMBURG
STOCKHOLM • ATHENS • TOKYO • MILAN • MADRID
PRAGUE • WARSAW • BUDAPEST • AUCKLAND

Kelsey, this one is for you.
You might be my oldest, but you'll always be my baby.

ISBN 0-373-69110-6

ROUGHING IT WITH RYAN

Copyright © 2003 by Jill Shalvis.

This edition published by arrangement with Harlequin Books S.A.

® and TM are trademarks of the publisher. Trademarks indicated with ® are registered in the United States Patent and Trademark Office, the Canadian Trade Marks Office and in other countries.

Visit us at www.eHarlequin.com

Printed in U.S.A.

1

SUZANNE CARTER glanced between the apartment-for-rent ads and the balance in her checkbook. No matter how much she squinted, added or subtracted, she was pretty much S.O.L.

With what she had, she'd be fortunate to get a place that had four walls and a roof, never mind such luxury items as hot water and a bathtub.

And yet, anything would be better than where she currently lived, which was nowhere. As of this morning, her fiancé—ex-fiancé, she reminded herself, her very ex-fiancé—had politely stacked her things outside the apartment they'd shared. Honest to God, she'd thought he'd been kidding.

Until her key hadn't worked. Seemed the joke was on her. Damn if the joke wasn't always on her.

In any case, she'd finally realized the truth. She was relationship cursed. If she hadn't been, then she could blame any one of her other ex-fiancés—there had been three in total, not that she was counting—for the relationship failures, but the fault was hers alone. She seemed to possess the single-handed ability to destroy a good man. She'd destroyed Tim to the point he'd cried every night, wanting her to talk about her feelings, *begging* her to open up. She'd felt horrible, but deep down she knew she didn't want a man who also cried at long-distance commercials and when he talked to his mother on the phone. Daily.

Not that Tim hadn't helped commit their relationship to doom by getting caught performing sexual gymnastics against the front door with his cleaning lady. But he'd pinned that on Suzanne as well, saying his heart had been so broken by her distance and lack of commitment that he'd needed the release.

Uh-huh.

This latest relationship disaster only confirmed in her own mind that she was cursed. And so, as of this moment, she was vowing to give up men to save them from herself. Too bad no one could save *her* from these dismal rental listings. Maybe she should have fought for the apartment, but she no longer wanted it. With a sigh she lifted her red pen and circled the very cheapest ad in the paper she could find. *That's right, get thrifty,* she could hear her mother say with approval. *And regimented.*

Everyone said Suzanne needed some regimentation. Well, everyone but her father, from whom she'd gotten her "lack of." Just ask her mother.

The ad she'd circled boasted a *cheap, cheap, cheap*

one bedroom/one bathroom walk-up. Cheap, cheap, cheap sounded right up Suzanne's alley, given that, one, she was currently homeless with no savings, and two, contrary to popular belief, chefs made next to nothing. Home Sweet Home, she thought, she *hoped*, and got in her car.

Being a Monday, South Village was hopping in a way she still couldn't get used to. When she'd been young, the area, just outside of Los Angeles, had been little more than an outdated, neglected area of commerce, the buildings all falling apart, the homeless camping on the corners. Then some historical committee had come along, and the next thing Suzanne knew, the place had incorporated and rebuilt itself, creating a delightful cosmopolitan area that people came from all over to visit.

It was considered *the* hot spot, filled with trendy cafés and restaurants, art galleries and unique shops, all designed to draw in urban singles by the BMW-load.

She managed to park her not-even-close-to-a-BMW at the correct address and pulled her sunglasses down her nose to get a better glimpse at the building. It didn't help. No matter how she looked at it, the view was the same.

Bad. The building's turrets, mock balconies and many windows, while charming, couldn't quite dis-

guise the fact that it needed major repairs—or demo-
lition.

However, this was South Village, which meant that
on either side of the falling-off-its-foundation-dump
sat beauty personified. For blocks in either direction,
all the other once decrepit old buildings had been re-
stored to their former glory.

Not that she could afford one of *those* places. But
that wasn't the point, she reminded herself. Today
was a new day, and a chance to prove to the world
she could do this without screwing up and without
bringing another man to ruin. This was her chance to
learn to be responsible and mature. To be regimented.

Which, really, by the age of twenty-seven, she
should have learned already. "So. It's come to this,"
she said to the building in front of her, and slid out of
her car.

The bottom floor appeared to be meant for com-
mercial use, though its glory days were long past.
There were two storefronts, with surprising potential
given the picture windows and brick work, but both
were vacant and dark, the area out front overgrown
with weeds.

Since the apartment listing read *walk-up*, she assumed she needed the second or third floor, and was
sort of hoping maybe she'd gotten the wrong place al-

together when the tree right next to her started to shake. It was an oak tree, full and majestic, one of many surrounding the building.

And it was shimmying and shaking like crazy.

In her next breath, a man dropped right out of the thing. And not some normal man either, but a tall, dark, leanly muscled man, and given his scowl, she could add *attitude-ridden* to the list.

Straightening his broad shoulders, she got a quick impression of wavy sable hair and deeply tanned features while he stared up at the tree. Still not noticing her, he shoved his sunglasses up on his head, then put his big hands against the huge trunk and... pushed?

Suzanne's gaze dropped from the back of his head to his now straining body in shocked curiosity. For the life of her, she couldn't look away.

He was beautiful.

Maybe beautiful was the wrong word, as it brought to mind female qualities and there was nothing feminine about this man and his superb form. Holy smokes, just looking at him, she needed a cup of ice to soothe her suddenly parched throat.

He wore faded Levi's over legs that went on forever, and a white T-shirt that was sorely stressing at the seams against his working muscles, of which he seemed to have plenty. Not that he was overbuilt, no sirree, not like a bodybuilder, who in her opinion was usually over the top. No, this man was more like a long, lean boxer.

Not that it mattered! My God, she was *so* done with men. Had she forgotten she destroyed them on a fairly regular basis? She didn't need yet another one on her conscience, thank you very much. But in spite of herself, her mouth dropped open a little as she took in his tough, sinewy back and shoulders, vibrating with power while he beat up this tree. He was quite determined about it, too.

But then he caught her staring. When he did, a smile crossed his face that transformed him from merely take-another-look to...*wow*.

"Sorry if I startled you," he said and scooped up a discarded clipboard. And because she was weak, and he was so...yummy, she stared at his butt while he bent over, then jerked her gaze upward when he straightened.

Bad girl.

He had tanned, rugged features that spoke of an outdoor life, and dark, dark eyes, with the sort of laugh lines fanning out from them that would so horrify a woman but looked so sexy on a man. He made a quick note on the clipboard, and, whistling now, turned and entered the building.

What had he said? *He was sorry to have startled her?*

Presumably because he'd dropped out of a tree like Tarzan.

If he only knew what had startled her was how he seemed to trigger everything feminine within her, despite the fact she wasn't interested.

Not at all. Not even one little bit. She had a life to fix, and regimentation to put into it. Lifting her chin, she put Gorgeous Crazy Tree Guy right out of her mind and entered the building as well.

"Hello?" she called out. Her voice echoed and it appeared she was alone.

Not a gorgeous crazy tree guy in sight.

Taking the stairs to the second floor, she found two doors—both locked—presumably leading to apartments. From above she heard voices, so she took the stairs to the third and final floor, which opened to a loft apartment.

She stepped into what was probably meant to be a living room, but the room was empty and as filled with dust as the hallway had been. It was also small, yet the picture window facing the street somehow made it okay. Sunshine streamed in fully to the wooden floor, and as the dust bunnies danced through the air, Suzanne could see the place had potential.

Because the kitchen was separated by only a mini-bar, she could see two people standing in the cramped space, huddled over a set of blueprints laid out on the counter. The woman had a hand to her mouth, deep in concentration. As Suzanne's sandals clicked across the floor, the woman looked up.

She appeared to be about Suzanne's age, only that's where the similarities ended. Unlike her own unruly Little Orphan Annie mop, this woman had glamour hair—blond and pulled back in a careful, elegant twist Suzanne could never manage to do for herself without pulling both arms out of their sockets. The woman also wore glamour makeup and glamour clothes to match. Surrounded by dust and the cramped loft, she looked as out of place as a princess on a frog's lily pad.

Suzanne might have dwelled on that, and the fact that *she* always wrinkled whether or not she stood absolutely still, except that the man looked up, too.

It was *him*. Gorgeous Crazy Tree Guy.

He looked right at her, his big body dwarfing the small space. Wouldn't you know it, his eyes were the perfect color of a double chocolate mocha—her favorite—and held an intensity that spoke of passion. She could have drowned in them.

If she hadn't given up men. Which she had. A shame really, because he definitely had a face designed to tempt women—sort of saint and sinner all packed into one very well put together unit.

"Hi," she said, a little self-consciously. "Is this the apartment marked in the paper as..." she unrolled the newspaper and quoted the ad, "Cheap, cheap, cheap?"

The woman laughed, not the snooty sound one might have expected either, and pushed at a nonexistent stray strand of hair with a long-fingered, well-manicured hand. "I hope that didn't turn you off."

"Are you kidding?" Suzanne pictured her own decidedly unhappy bank account. "It drew me here like a moth to the flame. How cheap exactly?"

"We'll talk. But first..." She turned to the man. "Can we finish this later?"

"Later is going to be too late, Taylor."

Suzanne should have guessed he'd have a tempting voice to go with that face, low and serrated and sexy. His face didn't hide feelings, and at the moment he appeared to be highly annoyed as he rolled up the plans.

If the woman was annoyed back, she had too much class to let it show. "I need a tenant."

"You need to fix those trees. Any one of them on the east side could blow over in the next good storm, which by the way, is due tonight."

"Ryan." She touched his arm, and Suzanne watched as the man gave in with a sigh.

Suzanne had never in her life tamed a man with

just a touch, much less a man like that—a big hulk of a man who wouldn't tame easily.

Was it the expensive clothes or the way the woman wore them, Suzanne wondered. Self-conscious, she ran her hand down her sundress, which was not only *not* in style with its long, flowing flowery skirt, but was wrinkled. She wore it because it hid her flaws, the biggest one being her fondness for her own cooking. A *great* fondness. As in ten extra pounds fondness.

"Relax, the weather channel is *never* right." Taylor patted the man's arm again. "Tomorrow will be soon enough to decide on the trees."

He shook his head, his dissatisfaction showing in the tension in his big body, in the heat radiating in those riveting eyes.

Fascinated in spite of herself, Suzanne watched him. The men in her life—the only one at present being her father—never showed their real feelings. In the Carter household intense emotion was the source of great amusement, and all adversity was met with laughter. Footloose and fancy-free, that was the Carter family motto. Her fiancés had followed a similar pattern, hiding their emotions behind masks, even Tim with his big, teary eyes disguising his cheating, manipulative ways.

And until right this very moment she'd never once realized there was any other way for a man to be.

Gorgeous Tree Guy—*Ryan*—brushed past her with an acknowledging nod. Their shoulders touched, his mouth curving slightly in apology.

Embarrassing to admit, but her pulse scrambled and she craned her neck to watch him go. Apparently deciding she was cursed and swearing off relationships didn't affect the lust genes from operating.

"Yeah." Taylor had come to stand beside her. "He's quite fine."

Suzanne agreed, but kept her opinion to herself.

"And though he's far too kind to show it, he's royally pissed at me at the moment." She gave an elegant shrug. "He'll live."

They both moved to the door to watch him vanish down the stairs, momentarily absorbed in the way his T-shirt so nicely outlined his wide shoulders and strong back, and then there were those jeans, so lovingly cupping his long, well-defined legs, not to mention the best-looking butt Suzanne had ever seen.

The woman standing next to her—looking far more suited for a fancy luncheon than standing in the dusty room—sighed lustily, then shrugged it off. "So. I'm Taylor Wellington. I placed the ad. Do you want the apartment?"

Suzanne might have utterly failed in the love department—*three* times—but she hadn't been born yesterday. "I think I should see the rest of it first."

"Oh. Yes, of course." Taylor took a look around her, then cut her gaze back to Suzanne's. "Just remember, it's cheap, okay? *Really* cheap. Now here's the bedroom, just off the front here." She opened a door that Suzanne had assumed was a closet.

It wasn't much bigger than one, but it did have a window to the street, where she could see an array of shops and galleries, and people walking up and down the sidewalks. It charmed her, and was infinitively better than sleeping in her car.

Then she caught the sign for the shop directly across the street and her heart leaped. "An ice-cream shop?"

"Open until 11:00 every night," Taylor confirmed. "You just keep that in mind now, as you look at the bathroom."

The bathroom was the size of a postage stamp. No tub, Suzanne thought with a sigh, but it had all the basics—a shower, a sink and a commode.

"Everything's in working order," Taylor promised. "That is if you don't try to make toast and use a hair dryer at the same time. And hey, with a good scrubbing, the place might even be cute. What do you think?"

"I think if the price is right, I'll take it."

"The price is right," Taylor promised. "Come with me downstairs, I have the forms. When would you move in?"

Suzanne thought of her belongings all wedged into her car. "I hope now is good."

Taylor laughed. "If you have first and last month's rent, plus a small security deposit, now is perfect."

Damn. "Uh...how attached to the security deposit idea are you?"

Nicole stopped and looked her over. "Hurting for cash?"

"You could say that." Tim had let her purchase his very expensive bedroom furniture with her savings several weeks ago. Furniture he now claimed had been her gift to him. Gift, ha! She could have fed a small country for a year on what she'd paid. Odd how mad that made her now, when she'd so happily given him everything only a month ago. "But I do have a job," she said positively, which was true. "Will that help?"

"Yes, a job is good." Taylor thought it over. "We can skip the deposit."

They started down the stairs again, Taylor in her fancy wear, looking like royalty visiting the slums, and Suzanne with her gypsy dress, fitting right into her immediate surroundings.

"What is it that you do?" Taylor asked.

"I'm a chef at Café Meridian." As Suzanne mentioned the café only about five blocks from this very spot, a flicker of unease rolled over her shoulders. She'd moved up from a less esteemed kitchen when Tim's sister had purchased the place and Tim had insisted Suzanne would love working for his sister. Now that they had broken up, Suzanne hoped it wouldn't be awkward to continue working there. Though she'd taken less money than she'd wanted to, she loved the job.

Okay, so she loved food. Period. But she needed the job. Without it, she'd have to rely on her catering, which was simply a hobby and would stay that way. Running a business would be...well, too regimented. Far too regimented.

Sorry, Mom.

Carters in general—meaning her and her dad—didn't do serious. Which was why her mother couldn't talk to either of them without her jaw getting all bunched up. Her father was still a struggling stand-up comedian at nearly sixty years of age. On the outside it looked like he was a slacker left over from an age when that was a good thing, but the truth was, he loved his carefree life. Material possessions and corporate success meant less to him than his freedom.

Suzanne, according to her mother, was a chip off the old block.

She and Taylor came to the second floor landing, where Taylor unlocked one of the two apartments, then gestured for Suzanne to enter. "This is my place."

Suzanne stood in the empty living room not so different from the one on the floor above, except this place had been cleaned spotless. "But it's...empty."

"I've just moved in myself, and into the bedroom only. The rest is a job for this week."

"You own the building?"

Taylor slid a very tasteful beige pump, which probably cost more than Suzanne's entire wardrobe, over the smooth floor. "I do now."

"Pardon my frankness, but you're dressed to the nines, dripping elegance and sophistication, and yet I have the strangest feeling that you don't have any more money than I do."

Taylor sighed and rolled her head on her neck. "What gave me away? The not wanting to put money into the trees?"

"Let's just say desperation recognizes desperation."

Taylor laughed. "You know what? I like you. Okay, here's the humiliating truth. I grew up with the proverbial silver spoon in my mouth—the best of schools, the whole works. College at Brown University, courtesy of Great-Grandpa's Swiss bank account. After graduation, I traveled Europe for fun."

"Also on Grandpa's Swiss bank account?" Suzanne guessed, and when Taylor nodded, she shook her head. "I'm not feeling sorry for you yet."

"I know, we're getting to that." Taylor lifted her hands in a surrendering gesture. "I was spoiled rotten, I admit it. I never worked a day in my life, never worried about money, nothing. Then Grandpa, who I only saw every few years when he felt the need to see firsthand how his money was paying off, up and died on me."

"How inconsiderate," Suzanne murmured.

"But he left me this building."

"It's prime real estate. It's got to be worth a fortune."

"Yeah, if you have a fortune to spend on it." Taylor grimaced. "He didn't leave me any money to go with it, not one single dime. I've never had to save money and I don't have a job so I'm flat broke."

"Except for this building."

"Except for this building," she agreed. "Obviously I need tenants, as I've found I'm rather fond of eating. I figure I can get cash flow from the rentals. And as it all starts to come in, I promise to fix the place up. If you want to help, I'll give you a break on the rent. So...still want the loft?"

Suzanne might have grown up with her comedian father, who thought everything was a joke, but she did have a brain. "Why not just sell and pocket the dough?"

Taylor vehemently shook her head. Not a single hair fell out of place. "Cave on my first real challenge? No way."

Suzanne felt herself let loose a genuine smile—her first since finding her belongings stacked in the hall and the locks changed. "You know, I think I like you back."

Taylor's return smile came slow and easy. "Good." There seemed to be relief in that smile. "Here are the rental forms. Just you, right?"

"Just me. Single forever, from this point on."

"Ah. Something else we have in common."

"I mean it. I'm..." What the hell. "I am relationship cursed."

Taylor laughed, then when Suzanne didn't, her laughter faded. "You're...not kidding."

"Not on this, believe me." She lifted a hand and made a solemn vow. "No matter what the temptation, I shall resist."

"I'm with you. No matter the temptation," Taylor agreed just as solemnly. "Even temptation in the form of a magnificent tree man with an ass that makes my knees weak."

Suzanne's lips twitched. "Even that." She signed on the dotted line.

"To us," the pretty blonde said, lifting an imaginary toast. "And a prosperous future all on our own. No men. Soon as I can afford it, I'll buy *real* champagne to toast with."

"To us," Suzanne agreed with a smile. "Good luck, Taylor."

"And to you, Suzanne."

Suzanne raised both her imaginary glass and her gaze to the ceiling, picturing her loft above.

Luck? She, for one, was going to need it.

2

RYAN ALONDO stood in his shower, head bent as the hot water beat down on his back. His hands braced on the wall kept his exhausted body vertical because he wasn't certain he could trust himself not to fall asleep right there on his feet. He stood that way until the hot water gave out and he turned off the flow of water.

And then found not a single towel in sight. *"Angel!"*

"I know, I know, I took the last clean towel." A giggle followed from just outside the bathroom door. "Sorry."

Great, she was sorry and he was bare ass naked. And cold.

Outside the small beveled window of the bathroom came the sounds of a whipping wind. A storm was definitely brewing but he was too tired to think about what that might mean to the countless property owners who had disregarded his recommendations that old trees be cut down before they blew down. Right now he just wanted to dry off, eat something and then sleep for a decade or two. Since no towel had materialized, he shoved his wet legs into his jeans, wincing when the thick denim clung to his wet body.

When he stepped out of the bathroom, Angel's voice came from the kitchen. "Your fridge is empty but I found a can of soup. I heated it up for you."

His fridge wouldn't be empty if she hadn't had friends over studying until all hours the night before, but he refrained from pointing that out because, as he walked into the kitchen, she was smiling at him.

As always, the heart he'd never learned to harden caved.

"I know it's a pain in your butt having your baby sister crash at your place," she said softly, watching him sit at the table and pull the bowl of soup closer. "But Russ and Rafe are such pigs I can't handle their place."

Their brothers *were* pigs, so he nodded and started eating. He was starving. But soup wasn't going to cut it, so he could only hope something more substantial still existed in his cupboards. Anything.

"Lana's place will be ready by the weekend, and I'll move in with her."

Ryan put down his spoon, and looked at his baby sister. She wasn't really a baby anymore at eighteen but as he'd practically raised her, it was a tough image to dispel. The baby sister he'd taught to read, slug a baseball out of the park and drive a car in between the dotted lines was going to move in with Lana, a fast, big-mouthed girl whose behavior made his jaw feel too tight. "I thought Lana had a live-in boyfriend," he said carefully when what he really wanted to say was "no way."

"She kicked him out."

Much as he wanted his own space back, including his clean towels, he wouldn't be able to sleep if he thought Lana's no-good boyfriend was around. "Promise?"

"Promise." From behind, Angel wrapped her arms around him and pressed her cheek to his. "You're cute when you're worried. I love you, Ryan."

He groaned. "Oh no, the I-love-you card. What do you need?"

She laughed in delight. "Nothing. For a change. Absolutely nothing."

Ryan crossed his arms, taking a stand with the only child/woman who'd ever bested him. "Nothing really? Or nothing, I don't want to tell you yet?"

"Nothing really." Her smile was indulgent. "You worry too much about us."

Sheer habit. Their parents had been little more than kids themselves when they'd had Ryan. "A blessed accident" his mother had called him. It had taken years for them to get established, which was why his three siblings hadn't started to come along until he'd been thirteen.

His parents had been deliriously happy with their late-in-life family, until they'd been killed in a car accident seven years ago. That had left twenty-five-year-old Ryan to raise an eleven-year-old Angel and twin twelve-year-old boys, Russ and Rafe. A nightmare by any standards.

"We're not lost little kids anymore, okay?" Angel said. "You can ease up on the overprotective thing."

He probably could, but raising all three of his siblings from teenagers, by some miracle getting each of them through those years without any unplanned pregnancies or drug addictions, he still felt...tense.

Kissing his cheek, Angel leaned over and grabbed the check he'd left for her on the table. "Thanks for my tuition and book money."

He shoveled in some more soup and grunted. God, he was tired. It was so bad his eyes were closing right there on the spot.

"Oh, Ryan, get some sleep tonight. No hot date, okay?" She patted the top of his head. "Unlike last night, I might add."

Last night he'd been at college, same as she, only on the other side of the campus, where he'd been feverishly attempting to finish the landscape architectural degree that would get him out of the tree business once and for all. Not that he had explained that to Angel or his brothers, which is why they believed him to be some sort of sex fiend who dated one woman or another three nights a week.

He could have told them the truth. After putting his life on hold for so long to take care of them, they'd understand and support him.

But for once, he wanted to do something alone, not by Alondo committee. As much as he loved his siblings, he didn't need their advice about courses, academic life or any other topic they considered themselves experts on. Plus there was the added bonus...if they believed him to be a wild man, they'd stop trying to set him up on disastrous blind dates. So far the plan had worked like a charm. "No hot date," he murmured. No class. Just his bed. Alone.

Heaven.

And it was that. So much so that when he finally crawled under his sheets, practically whimpering with gratitude, he was out before his head hit the pillow.

And stayed out until he woke with a jerk when the phone rang at one o'clock in the damn morning.

Sorely tempted to ignore it, he stared at the offending receiver. Sleep was trying to tug him back under, but it could be Russ or Rafe, in some sort of trouble.

Or worse, Angel, in need of his help. "Better be good," he said in lieu of a greeting.

"Ryan?"

Not Russ, not Rafe. Not Angel.

"Ryan, it's Taylor Wellington."

And not the police or hospital, thank you God, just Taylor, the woman with the nightmare oak trees. He'd been surprised, and quite honestly disappointed, when she hadn't seen the urgency of her own situation. After all, *she'd* called *him*, greeted him in an outfit that cost more than his truck, then turned her nose up at his price to take down the trees, which had been damn reasonable, if he said so himself. "Taylor...is everything all right?"

"No. Remember that tree you warned me about?"

"Which one?"

"All of them, but most importantly the one on the east side of the building. It just fell on my roof and through the loft apartment's bedroom. I really need you to clear it. Now."

That particular tree had been at least one hundred years old, massive and severely damaged from the last few Santa Ana winds. The sheer size of the thing had worried Ryan, with good reason apparently. "At least the apartment is empty."

"*Was* empty. Tonight it has my new roommate in it,

Suzanne, the woman you saw me interviewing today."

The image of Suzanne flashed through Ryan's mind—long, wavy, dark-red hair, a lush, generously curved body beneath a flowing sundress. Crystals hanging from her ears, and the biggest, greenest, most expressive eyes he'd ever seen.

There'd been awareness in those eyes, an awareness he might have been interested in, if his life could handle one more interest. Now dread filled him. "Is she—"

"She's okay, but the way the tree fell, it's blocking her way out."

"I'm on my way," he promised and hung up the phone, only to immediately lift it again to wake up his crew, made up of Rafe and Russ, his two younger, very groggy twin brothers. At least they'd been in their apartment, alone and available, he thought with relief, racing for his truck. Old habits were hard to break, which meant he still felt like mom, dad, boss and older brother all at the same time—too many hats for any one person.

He lost five minutes stopping at his office, but if he was going to be pulling a tree off a building, he needed the big rig from the yard there.

As he switched trucks, rain slashed through his

clothes, aided by a vicious wind that wouldn't help him tonight.

She's okay, Taylor had said, but the devastating possibilities made him go as fast as he dared. South Village was deserted, unusual for the trendy streets, even at this hour. The storm had sent everyone scampering home.

When he finally pulled up in front of the building, his stomach tightened. The huge old oak had indeed hit the roof. And as Taylor had said, just the far east corner, which was both good and bad. Good, because the main structure and all three floors were intact. Bad, because the crash impacted the loft apartment, specifically the bedroom, where according to Taylor, Suzanne was at this very moment. The window was gone, blown out, as well as the entire left half of the front wall, where the tree protruded obscenely.

Ryan squinted past the downpour and squeezed the arm of a worried Taylor, who stood on the porch in a silk lounging robe, looking as absolutely glamorous at one in the morning as she had twelve hours earlier.

"Her bedroom door is blocked," she said, gripping the edges of her robe tight against the wind, staring through the stormy night to the destroyed window three stories above them. "The way the tree fell, she can't get out."

"We'll get her."

"Hurry. And Ryan," she added when he turned away to get to work. "I'm sorry. So sorry I didn't listen to you."

"It'll be okay," he said. And hoped he could make it so.

His crew went to work, and when the rig ladder had been set parallel to the fallen tree, Ryan started climbing. Rain and wind whipped his face and body, but if he felt unnerved, he could only imagine what poor Suzanne was feeling, and he climbed faster. From below, Rafe directed a spotlight, highlighting Ryan's way.

When he got to the top, he could understand why Suzanne hadn't been able to get out. The tree had fallen diagonally across her bedroom, trapping her in the far corner of the room, away from both the blown-out window and the door.

He was at the hole now, but the massive trunk and branches blocked his view. Craning his neck, he tried to see past the dark and the driving rain and all the drenched greenery. He moved from the ladder to the ledge, wedging his body in with the tree.

Still couldn't see a damn thing. "Suzanne?"

"H-here!"

Hunkering down, he was able to crawl on his belly beneath the trunk, ignoring the sharp branches scratching his arms and back. He slicked the rain from his face, and still couldn't see her. Where was she?

A sudden female sneeze gave him his answer, and he moved forward until he saw ten toes. Pulling himself up, Ryan squeezed into the cramped little space with her, letting out a pent-up breath because she was here. Alive.

She'd indeed found the one small safe haven available to her, and as he pulled the flashlight from his belt and turned it on, his heart clenched. She was huddled, back to the wall, knees to her chest, her arms wrapped tight around her legs.

Careful of the broken glass, he shifted up to his knees. "Suzanne? You okay?"

Her long hair, wet from the blowing rain, clung to her head and shoulders as she gave him a jerky nod paired with a shudder. She relaxed her position slightly, not huddling quite so tightly.

Her arms and legs gleamed in the glow of the flashlight, bare and also wet. No longer dressed in her long, flowing sundress and crystals, she wore only a tank top and a pair of panties, and even as he looked her over for injuries, trying not to linger on the way the material clung to her breasts or the way her nipples were so clearly defined, she continued to shake. The hem of the tank top didn't meet her panties, showing him the smooth skin of her belly. It quivered with her every shallow breath, whether from fear or cold, he didn't know. It didn't matter.

Reacting only to the fact she was shaking so violently—probably in shock, damn it—he simply put down the light and pulled her close.

3

SUZANNE DOVE INTO Ryan's long, strong arms, nearly whimpering in gratitude. Despite the fact he was as wet as she, warmth radiated off his body. She felt like a heat-seeking missile, burrowing close, then closer still, not caring at the moment that she didn't know him from Adam.

Later she'd worry what he'd thought of her when she crawled up his big, hard body and pressed her face to his throat. Later she'd worry about her less than half-dressed state, or that she'd arched her body to a perfect stranger's in mindless terror. Later.

But for right now, never more thankful to see another living soul, she just closed her eyes against the storm blasting through the broken window, wrapped her arms around him tight as she could, and held on through the wild tremors that shook her body in uncontrollable waves.

He made a rough sound of wordless comfort and pressed her closer. In spite of the urgency of the situation, she became startlingly aware of him and how he felt plastered to her. And how he felt was... incredible.

The wind continued to blow, bringing in more cold rain and the tinkling sound of glass scattering over the floor. "The glass from the window," he murmured in her ear, and slipping an arm beneath her, he lifted and turned her so that she lay in his lap, his body hunched over hers, protecting her from the elements the best he could. As a gesture, it was the sweetest one that anyone had ever made for her. But the sweetness contrasted sharply with the decidedly *not* sweet feelings making themselves known within her.

"Are you cut?" His voice was hoarse with worry, probably because she was staring at him like an idiot—as she sat there realizing her best intentions to stay away from men for their own good were about to fail.

"Suzanne?"

Still shaking—though now she wasn't sure it was all from the cold—she shook her head.

He cuddled her closer, one hand on her still quivering belly, his face only an inch away. His gaze burned into hers, dark and intense. "Are you sure?"

The shivers had really taken over her body now, so she nodded. Weak with relief and fear, it was about all she could do.

Clearly not willing to take any chances in the dark, he reached for the flashlight on the floor at his hip and ran it over her, looking for himself.

She glanced down and saw what he saw... Her wet, clinging, now thoroughly see-through tank and panties, both of which had risen to levels they shouldn't have, both of which revealed her in all her unwieldy glory, and she slammed her eyes shut.

"It's okay," he whispered roughly, clearly mistaking her movement for fear. Holding her close, he cupped her head in his big hand. "You're okay. Let's get you out of here, how does that sound?"

"I—I'll be f-f-fine."

"Oh yeah, you will." Still holding her, he used his free hand to lift a radio to his mouth.

Because her ears seemed to be ringing, she didn't quite catch the conversation. Exhausted, she set her head on his chest, which allowed her to feel the vibration of his deep voice, and for some reason, it was horribly seductive. He smelled good, her sexy hero. And Lord, he felt good, too.

How had this happened? One moment she'd been in a deep slumber, dead to the world. The next she'd been startled right out of that sleep by the loudest crack of thunder she'd ever heard, followed immediately by another crack, not from Mother Nature this time, but from the tree.

She'd leapt off the mat Taylor had let her borrow, just as the tree crashed through the ceiling and window.

Overwhelmed by the near-miss, a little stunned that she was alive, she'd sat there until she'd heard Taylor's frantic voice calling for her.

Now she'd been rescued by the man who'd so mesmerized her earlier, the most amazing, strong, sexy man she'd ever laid eyes on.

But he was *just* a man.

And for better or worse, she'd sworn off the entire species. She'd even vowed so to Taylor. Handy that vow, as without it, her resolve might have been weakened by the feel of his rock solid, incredibly warm body against hers.

A flash of blinding lightning lit the room, and with it came an accompanying boom of thunder that seemed to echo inside her head, making her act impulsively, which meant she tried to crawl up Ryan's body.

He hugged her. "We're getting out of here, I promise."

She gave a jerky nod, and he rewarded her with a gentle squeeze of his hands. "In the meantime," he said. "Pretend you're somewhere else, anywhere... like your nice, toasty bed, fast asleep, okay?"

She could imagine the bed part, if he was in it.

No. Bad girl. Bad, bad.

"Anywhere," he repeated, his voice like silk in her ear. "Name it."

"Well..." She cleared her rough throat. "When I'm stressed, I..."

"You what?"

"I...eat ice cream."

"Ice cream?"

"Yeah. I could really use a gallon about now."

He let out a bark of laughter. "An entire gallon, huh? That's good, that's real good. Make it chocolate and I'll join you. Deal?"

She lifted her head and blinked into the dark until she could almost see his expression. A man who'd eat chocolate ice cream out of the gallon with her? He had to be saying that just to fool her, no man was that astute. "You like chocolate ice cream out of the container?"

His hands on her had been nothing but light. Comforting. But now, while their gazes were locked, his hands seemed more than just protective, they seemed...hungry. "A beautiful woman asks me to share a delicious dessert with her?" He smiled a smile that made her hormones stand up and beg. "I'd eat bugs on a stick."

Her last fiancé would have scrunched up his face and "how unsanitary." Her first fiancé would have known exactly how many calories and fat grams that would have equaled. Not this man, her hero. He'd do anything to make her feel safe.

A flash of lightning fully illuminated Ryan's face an instant before a crack of thunder hit. At the sound her body jerked. Ryan slid his hands up her arms to cup her face. "Shh," he whispered, his thumb tracing the line of her lower lip. "We're getting out of here. Right now, okay?"

She stared at the tree stuffed into what had been her new bedroom. The tree that blocked her door. Knowing she was three stories up, and that he hadn't flown to get here, she swallowed hard and tried not to panic. "We're going to go the way you came in, I suppose."

"Yep." He lifted some branches, illuminating with his flashlight the way he'd come in. "If we go through here about eight feet, we'll come to the window."

Or what used to be her window.

Up on his knees now, he unbuttoned his long-sleeved chambray shirt and stripped it off, leaving him in a dark colored T-shirt. "I'm sorry it's wet, but it's better than nothing."

While she shoved her arms in the sleeves—grateful the hem came down to her thighs and more grateful for the body heat still in it—he said, "I'm going first so I can sweep away glass shards as we go. Stay close." Even though it was dark she could still see his intense gaze and the worry in it as he looked at her.

That concern cloaked her in strength, and fueled her own. She could do this. And yet she wished he'd touch her again, for comfort, for... She could still feel his fingers on her jaw. Could imagine them sinking into her hair—

"Suzanne?"

"Ready," she said quickly before he thought she was having a meltdown. If she was in danger of a meltdown, it was one of the senses, not of fear.

But how could she explain to herself the panic she suddenly felt wasn't due to the storm at all, but instead was due to the fact that she could feel her heart thumping painfully at the touch of this incredibly appealing stranger? She didn't want this adrenaline rush that signified awareness of him as a man. She didn't!

He tugged her hand until she was on her knees facing him, and at the reassuring look in his eyes, she swallowed hard. She knew he would do whatever he had to in order to keep her safe. It made her knees weak. It made her yearn, when she'd promised herself no more yearning.

"We'll be out of here before you know it." Another harsh crack of thunder reverberated through their small space, and Suzanne just about plowed him over in her haste to follow him.

"That's it," he murmured. "Stay close."

Stay close? She'd be on top of him if she could. On her hands and knees, she crawled after him, under the fallen tree, squinting against the howling wind, thinking her life was literally in the hands of this man in front of her.

Which really explained her odd reaction to him, she decided. Fear and adrenaline were powerful emotions. No doubt, in the light of day things would be back to normal. She'd go to work, balance her checking account, figure out if she had any money this week to start buying furniture—

Boom.

The thunder startled the breath right out of her, but Ryan was right there, helping her out from under the branches, slipping an arm around her waist. "Hey, just Mother Nature moaning and bitching. We're okay."

They were okay. Good. Okay was good. She lifted her head and found his mouth only an inch from hers.

He had a wide, firm mouth, and she suddenly, inanely wondered...did it know how to pleasure a woman?

His eyes were dark, gazed locked on to hers. Oh yeah, she thought shakily. He knew.

Oh, God, where were these inappropriate thoughts coming from? They were coming from her own desire, a desire she didn't understand. As she realized it, in the dim glow of the night, she saw the dangerous flare of a mirroring desire in his eyes.

And for a long heartbeat, neither of them moved.

"You ready?" he finally asked.

"Yeah. I'm...ready."

His gaze shifted to her mouth, he slowly nodded. "We're just going to climb through the opening and get onto the ladder."

Right. Climb through the opening and onto the ladder. "Got it."

The next flash of lightning, immediately followed by a bone-rattling boom of thunder came so suddenly after the stillness, they both jerked.

"Oh, God," she whispered a little tearfully, her heart in her throat. "I really could use that ice cream."

"I wish I had some." The thunder continued to echo around them. "But as far as distraction goes," he murmured. "I do have this." Lifting her against him, he surrounded her with his heat, his strength, before closing his mouth over hers.

Her hands fisted in his hair, looking for balance in a world where there was suddenly none to be had.

His kiss was glorious, made more so by the dark of the night, by the wet of the storm, by the lingering fear and adrenaline.

But then he slowly pulled back. Suzanne just barely managed not to cry out her protest. Through the darkness she could hear his ragged breathing—a ragged breathing that matched her own—as he stared at her and it was all she could do not to yank him back to her. Just as that thought formed in her mind, he lowered his head again, brushing his mouth over hers, almost in a question. She answered by slanting her mouth to better fit his, and then with a grateful, mutual groan, they sank into another wet, hot, long kiss.

With all that had happened to her already that night, a mere kiss shouldn't have been able to send more sensation rocketing through her, but that's exactly what it did. And then he was looking down at her, his breath coming hard and fast, a sort of stunned wonder on his face that she knew matched her own.

While she stood there, dizzy and weak-kneed and hot-blooded all at the same time, he ran a finger over her jaw, then turned back to the chore of getting them out.

SUZANNE FIGURED going down the ladder in Ryan's flapping shirt and little else, being greeted by his crew, a freaked out Taylor and the fire truck that had come to help, would headline her nightmares for some time to come.

But when it was over, less than an hour had passed since she'd been awakened by the tree hitting her bedroom.

A horrified Taylor insisted Suzanne share her own second story apartment, which had not been touched by the storm. There was no electricity, but with the flashlight Ryan had given her, she had no trouble seeing Taylor's bedroom, and the finery in it. The bed was a four poster king that even she, in all her antique ignorance, knew had to be worth a hefty fortune.

"I know," Taylor said, her voice husky with exhaustion. "I'm cash poor and asset rich. Stupid, huh? I could sell this stuff and get rid of the nation's debt." She looked around, a sadness in her eyes that said there was far more to her story than she'd let on. "After spending so much time searching and buying it all...I just can't. I love the pieces too much." She shrugged off the melancholy and shoved what looked like very expensive, very silk pajamas into Suzanne's hands. "Here, take these things and help yourself to a hot shower. Or I could draw you a bubble bath, if you'd rather."

"Oh, no, I—"

"And while you're soaking, I'll fix you a snack—"

"Taylor—"

"Do you like cheese and crackers? I have some wine—"

"Taylor." She smiled into Taylor's pensive features. "I'm okay. Really. I'm not going to sue you or anything."

Surprising her, Taylor suddenly sagged a little, then grabbed Suzanne close in a fierce bear hug that sucked the oxygen right out of her. "Do you think I care about money?" she asked in a horrified whisper. "My God, you're my friend and my attempts at cost-cutting nearly got you killed tonight."

A little flustered, Suzanne pulled back. "Friend?"

"We bonded over our singlehood together, didn't we? Do you think I do that with just anyone?" Abruptly, Taylor turned away. Wrapping her arms around herself, she stared out into the dark, stormy night. "I'm so sorry, Suzanne. I'll never forgive myself for what happened tonight, for what could have happened."

"But I'm okay. Taylor, look at me." Suzanne held out her arms, still wearing Ryan's shirt. It smelled like him, and for a moment she remembered exactly what it had felt like to be held by the man who owned that delicious one-hundred-percent male scent. "Not a scratch on me."

"Are you going to leave?"

"Well...it might be hard to live in a loft without a roof."

"You can take the apartment next to mine."

"That's very sweet, but these units are twice as big. I'm sure I can't afford it."

"You can, because I'm going to give it to you for the same price as the loft. This month free of course, as reimbursement for what happened tonight. Please Suzanne, please stay."

The thought of finding another place exhausted her, but she felt as if she was taking advantage of the situation. "Taylor—"

"It's important to me. Already *you're* important to me."

It had been a very long time since someone had wanted her around, *really* wanted her around. Oh, her family loved her, she was certain. But they didn't show love easily, if at all. And lately, true to Carter form, she'd followed suit, drifting from one relationship to another, making sure to ruin the men emotionally before she got too attached.

This strange bond with Taylor threw her because of its immediate depth, and yet it made her feel good at the same time. "Thank you," she said simply.

"Is that a yes?"

"It's a thank God, yes, I want to stay." Suzanne let

out a sheepish smile. "I don't really care to see how warm I can get my car right now."

Taylor let out a grateful smile, then bustled Suzanne into the shower.

BY THE TIME Suzanne stepped out of the bathroom and back into the bedroom, there was hot cocoa waiting.

"Don't get used to this," Taylor warned. "I'm far more used to being served than being the server." She slipped into one side of the bed, leaving Suzanne with enough room on her side for a small army.

Climbing into bed required the last of her depleted energy. She pulled up the silky sheets and weighty blanket, grateful for the warmth. "It would be a shame to sell this bed. It's so luxurious."

"I know, but with it, and all the other antiques I have in storage, I could start the renovations."

"Wow, that's terrific." Suzanne felt awed by the collector's spirit, something she'd never personally experienced. Somehow her lifestyle to date made it easier to travel light.

"It's been a terribly expensive hobby," Taylor admitted, fluffing her pillows. "And one I can no longer afford, obviously. But no worries. First thing tomorrow we'll get you down from the loft and into the apartment next door. Then after Ryan is done with the tree extraction, I'll start on everything else. I'll need an architect, a contractor—"

"Ryan." Just the sound of his name had Suzanne wide awake again. She'd never again think of him as just the Gorgeous Crazy Tree Guy. He'd become her hero. And as such, a man to avoid at all costs. He was tempting enough to make her forget her vow to remain single and she wouldn't be able to live with herself if she destroyed her hero like she'd destroyed her ex-fiancés. "He's going to be around then?"

"All week, I imagine, getting that tree out and the others down."

All week. Would he talk to her in that voice of his, the one that said she was the only woman he saw? Would he touch her with those warm, sure hands? Or better yet, would he lean in and put that incredible mouth back on hers...?

Oh, boy, there it went again, her vivid imagination. She didn't want this inexplicable attraction. No sirree. She didn't need anyone or anything but herself and her chef job.

No matter how much her tingly nipples told her otherwise.

4

IT HAD BEEN JUST A KISS.

That's what Ryan told himself. All night long.

But he wouldn't have felt "just a kiss" from his head to his toes.

And let's not forget all the hot spots in between.

Sure, there were plenty of logical reasons for the almost chemical-like attraction between himself and Suzanne, two perfect strangers. For one, the situation itself had been terrifying. Obviously, that had played a big role in what had happened between the two of them up there in that loft, trapped alone on a dark, stormy night.

But somehow he knew, deep in his gut, the instant connection he'd felt with her couldn't be blamed on the events of the evening. Nor could the way he would have done anything—*anything*—just to keep her safe.

Unrested, and oddly driven to see her again in the light of day, he woke his crew at dawn. Not difficult as they were crashed on his couch.

When he flipped on the lights in the living room,

Russ groaned and buried his face into the couch cushion. "Five more minutes, Mom."

Mom had been gone for seven years. In fact, it had been Ryan to wake up his younger brothers for school every morning since, and still, no matter how much time went by, Russ, not a morning person, always talked to Mom first.

Ryan hauled the blankets off the nineteen-year-old, and did the same to Russ's twin, Rafe, who'd sometime in the night fallen to the floor and stayed there. "There's hot oatmeal and coffee," he told them. "Hurry, we've got a full day ahead."

"We just went to bed," Rafe whined.

"And now we're getting up."

"Donuts would be better." Rafe stumbled to the bathroom. After a moment he poked his head back out. "We saving any pretty redheads today?"

Ryan kicked the already back-to-sleep Russ's feet off the couch. "The only thing in your future today is a tree. A big tree. Our white knightship is over."

"Ah, man." Russ sat up and scrubbed his hands over his face, then suddenly brightened. "Hey! Don't wear a shirt today, just in case."

"In case what?"

"In case the pretty redhead decides to get wet in a tank and panties again." Russ grinned wickedly. "If you don't have a shirt to give her, then..." His eye-brows jerked up and down suggestively.

Ryan hauled the covers off him. "Get up, you per-vert." He strode toward the kitchen. "And as for making fun of last night, she could have died up there in that loft."

"Jeez, Ryan, I was just kidding." Russ stood and stretched. "But you can't blame a guy for dreaming about the way she looked all wet and—" When Ryan stopped and sent him an intensely black look, Russ closed his mouth. "I'm going to eat now."

"Good idea." Ryan went into the kitchen, leaned against the counter and closed his eyes, because he needed to think about something other than the im-age Russ had just put back in his brain. The one of Suzanne, drenched, with her clothes—his shirt—molded to her every curve, of which she had damn plenty.

"You like her or something?" Russ asked, follow-ing him. "Because you seemed awfully into her last night."

His siblings put an enormous amount of energy into finding Ryan a woman. It didn't take a genius to understand they wanted him happy. Which is why he pretended to date while actually going to college, just to keep them off his back. But as Suzanne seemed to have blindsided him with a genuine attraction he hadn't felt in a very long time, he didn't want to talk about it. Or her. "What I'm into," he said, "is getting to work. Today."

"Okay, okay. You're awfully touchy this morning."

Yeah, he was. And that he couldn't seem to help it disturbed him more than he would ever have admitted.

THE STORM HAD MOVED ON as fast as it had come, leaving the Southern California day beautiful and glistening. Ryan drove, listening to his brothers chatter about some party they were going to go to that night. South Village traffic was light at seven o'clock in the morning, although there were lots of pedestrians about. A woman jogging past in short shorts and a sports bra caused both Rafe and Russ to bump their faces against the window as they craned their respective necks trying to get a better view.

"Grow up," Ryan muttered, thinking he should have had another cup of coffee.

"If growing up means not looking at a chick like that, then no thank you."

"Shut up, Rafe." Russ gave Ryan a long worried look. "What's the matter?"

"What? Nothing."

"It's something for you to not look at a beautiful woman," he insisted. "You always look. Hell, then you sleep with half of them."

That wasn't exactly true. Not even partially true.

Okay, maybe partially true. In his twenties he'd been somewhat of a—

"Slut," Rafe said proudly. "I want to be just like you."

If they only knew. Between keeping the business going so he could feed everyone, and going to school, he was too tired to be a "slut." Half the time he was too tired to even *think* about sex. Sorry state for a thirty-two-year old. "Not everything revolves around sex."

"Yes it does," Russ said, and Rafe laughed.

They pulled up to the jobsite. Surveying the damage of the fallen tree in the light of day, Ryan let out a slow whistle. Last night they'd simply gotten Suzanne out and put supports under the fallen tree to protect the building from further damage. Getting that baby off the building was going to be tricky. To get a better feel for what had to be done, he climbed a ladder alongside the trunk of the tree. Halfway up, he paused to put on his work gloves, and then went utterly still.

He had a good view into the second floor window,

which was apparently a bedroom, given that he was looking at the largest bed he'd ever seen.

And in it, together, were two sleeping females.

Taylor and Suzanne.

MORNINGS WERE not Suzanne's thing. She'd rather be tortured on the rack than have to leap out of bed. And yet given the persistent stab of sunlight against her lids, she could surmise she needed to do exactly that if she wanted to get to the restaurant in time for the start of her shift.

Slowly she opened her eyes, keeping the rest of her body still. She'd sell her soul for coffee. Or cold pizza.

Yet somehow she doubted Taylor had cold pizza in her fridge.

As Suzanne's eyes focused, she could see Taylor still slept, looking as disgustingly put together and gorgeous as ever. How did the woman do that, hardly messing up a hair on her head during sleep? It was nothing short of amazing. If she wasn't so damn generous and giving, Suzanne would have hated her on principle.

Her gaze wandered to the window. Instead of the Los Angeles skyline smudged by smog, she saw a pair of wide shoulders, and a broad chest silhouetted by the sun, topped by the face that had headlined her dreams all night long.

Ryan.

With the sun behind him, she couldn't see his expression, but she could feel the tension in his big body, and knew he could see her much more clearly than she could see him. Beneath the luxurious covers, her body tingled, coming to the state of awareness she was beginning to associate with him. Lifting her hand, she waggled her fingers at him.

He mirrored the gesture, adding a crooked smile that somehow replaced her need for coffee, and continued his way up the ladder. She caught a flash of flat belly, lean hips, then long, long legs, before he vanished completely, leaving her to her own thoughts.

Thoughts that were suddenly far, far away from work and the day ahead. Thoughts that took her back to how she'd felt in his arms.

EXTRACTING THE TREE was physically intensive work. Ryan stopped to call for extra help from a labor pool he shared with some local contractors, and hoped like hell he got skilled guys.

As always on a big job, he worried about Rafe and Russ, but they were holding their own, directing the other crew members with such knowledge and authority Ryan felt a burst of pride.

He also felt regret. Yes, Rafe was going to college part-time, but Russ had taken the semester off, and

Ryan worried that he'd never get them both through it.

He didn't want them to be tree guys, as he'd been forced to be. As their father had been before him. He wanted so much more for them, but the truth was, they simply loved the work. How ironic was that, the business he'd worked at simply to keep a roof over their heads had become both the means and the end. Would it be such a bad thing if Russ and Rafe took over the business?

Wondering what he was supposed to do with that, he caught sight of a quickly moving female off to the side. A redheaded female.

Suzanne was racing out of the building toward her car, her hair loose and flowing past her shoulders. She wore some sort of gauzy skirt and matching sleeveless blouse, with bracelets up one arm that jangled as she ran.

Not much of her amazingly lush body showed—not that he was noticing. In fact, he tried mightily not to look too hard.

And failed.

"Caught ya," Rafe whispered in his ear. Laughing, he clapped his brother on the shoulder.

Ryan ignored Rafe for the moment and kept watching Suzanne, who hurried along, her breasts moving in a gentle bounce beneath her blouse. She slipped into her car and revved out into the street as if she had a fire on her tail. Her very fine tail, which Ryan happened to know looked unbelievably hot in white bikini panties. "That's Suzanne," he said.

"I know who she is. The sexy babe we rescued last night."

Sexy? Hell, yeah, and he was going to have to deal with that. He just didn't like Rafe thinking it.

The taillights of Suzanne's car disappeared. At least she didn't appear to be suffering any ill effects from last night.

"Ryan?"

"Yeah?"

"Take a picture, it'll last longer."

That snapped him out of it. What the hell was he doing, staring after her like a love struck teenager? For God's sake, he needed another person in his life like...like he needed a hole in his head.

But there was no denying she drew him, at least at the base lust level. She drew him, and he wanted to see it through.

"She looks good dry, too," Rafe said lightly. "Hey, with your busy dating schedule, how are you going to fit her in?" With another laugh, Rafe went back to work.

How was he going to fit her in? Ryan had no idea,

but suddenly, he knew without a doubt that he would.

"Ryan?"

Still shaken by that latest thought, he turned and faced Taylor, who came out of the building wearing some snazzy number that had every man within two square miles losing brain cells.

"I just dealt with the insurance agent," she said, lifting a hand. "So bear with me, I'm feeling pissy."

He nodded. "Join the club."

She smiled, but her voice was pure culture. "Can I be frank with you?"

"Of course."

"I know you think I'm a terrible person for allowing last night to happen." She stopped him when he would have spoken. "Please, let me say this. The truth is, I couldn't—can't—afford this place. I inherited it, with no cash to fix it up. And despite appearances..." She lifted her arms out, indicating her own expensive attire. "I have no income, at least not for the foreseeable future."

"This doesn't bode well for me getting paid," he said lightly.

"You'll get paid. I think I've figured out how to get some quick cash, so let's go ahead and trim back those other trees you were worried about as well, and

I'll have your money by the end of next week. I hope
that's okay, because—"

"It's okay." He managed a smile even though he
was still flummoxed over the realization he intended
to see Suzanne again, and soon.

"Are you sure?" Taylor asked.

Hell, half his clients didn't pay him until he threatened legal action. The end of the week would be just
fine. "Don't worry, we'll make you safe. In any case,
the worst is certainly over."

Taylor studied the building so desperately in need
of renovation. Her worried frown didn't fade. "Let's
hope so."

5

SUZANNE DROVE HOME from the Café Meridian on autopilot, numb from shock. She was unemployed. How could that be? Lately, her life seemed to be a really bad comedy—only she wasn't laughing.

Some of that numbness wore off as she parked in front of the building she'd promised not to move out of yet had no means to pay for.

Work removing the tree was underway, leaving the front yard of the building little more than a mountain of fallen branches and wood rounds. Men moved around, intense and concentrating. Not surprisingly, Suzanne's eyes honed right in on one in particular. Ryan.

Even from a distance, he had an authoritative quality to him as he worked, talked, coaxed, gestured. There was just something in his movements that set him apart, made her stomach quiver with recognition—and more.

Still walking, still gesturing, he turned, vibrant and charismatic, and lost in the passion of his work.

Ryan.

He wore denim and cotton, same as everyone else, but he didn't look like anyone else. His chest was broad, his arms well toned, his belly flat and corded. Muscles, muscles everywhere, she thought, a little dazed. And every one of those muscles was in defined relief as he moved in and around the fallen tree, calling out orders, picking up a saw, bending over a large branch himself.

The oak tree had been pulled off the building and lay across the front of the yard, looking almost harmless as the crew of men worked on it with chainsaws.

Harmless, ha! Given the gaping hole left in the wall—her wall—the loft apartment would be out of commission for a good while. Suzanne felt bad for Taylor, but it was hard to concentrate on that with her own life in the toilet.

And now that she was no longer numb—thank you lust hormones, and thank you Ryan, *not*—she vibrated with anger over what had just happened to her at work. Fingers shaking, she tore her gaze off Ryan's body and went through her purse for her cell phone. She found a pen out of ink, her plain Chap Stick and a half-burned vanilla votive candle, but no cell phone. Dumping out the contents of her purse, she pushed aside her unpaid Visa bill and a letter from ex-fiancé number two, begging her to try again, and *finally* located the phone. She could only hope she had an operating battery.

She did, but there was no reception. Great, because heaven forbid anything go her way today. She got out of her car, not forgetting to grab the bag with the gallon of ice cream she'd helped herself to from the café.

But still no reception.

Eye on the digital readout, she kept moving. Every few feet she paused, waiting, her rarely indulged redheaded temper gaining speed the longer the phone refused to work.

She backed up, moved to the side, even stomped her foot, and *finally* her phone obediently beeped its working status. Punching in the number for her ex's office, she sat on a round of wood and opened the bag with the ice cream. She'd thought ahead to grab a spoon as well, and had just taken her first mouthwatering bite of decadent double-fudge chocolate ice cream when Tim came on the line.

"Suzanne." His voice was kind. His voice was always kind, which now that she thought about it, annoyed the hell out of her. Did he have any other feelings like anger or frustration?

"What can I do for you?" he asked.

What could he do for her? Die a horrible, painful death, for starters. "Tim, I thought you were okay with our break-up."

"Well...I still miss you, you know that. I'll always miss you."

A load of dog poop, as she knew damn well from his sister that he had moved on from boinking the cleaning lady to boinking his secretary. "If that's true, why did you—"

"Suzanne? *Hello?* You still there?"

"Yes! I'm here. Tim, you—"

"You're breaking up. Hello? *Hello?*"

Damn it, she could hear him loud and clear. She was going to break *him* up. Instead, she tucked the ice cream container under her arm, stood and backed through the yard a little further. *There.* "The reception is fine," she said through her teeth. "So please, tell me why you've decided to wreck my entire life."

"A little melodramatic, don't you think?"

"What?" In the Carter fashion, she laughed in the face of emotion. Better they see you laugh than cry. "Melodramatic? No, I'm not being melodramatic. But I can give you melodramatic if you'd like." She stopped to shove a huge bite of slightly melted ice cream into her mouth. She almost groaned with pleasure at the rich flavor, but dragged her mind back to the task at hand. "Why did you get me fired?"

"Oh, that. It was too painful for me to know you were working at my sister's restaurant. I could never go there without being reminded of the emotional distance, the break-up...so I found someone else better suited for it, that's all."

"*What?* You found a better chef than me? Who?"

"Someone who will love me the way I deserve."

She winced. "Tim, what does *that* have to do with cooking?"

"It's my new girlfriend. She's thrilled, so thrilled she promised me all sorts of favors."

"You— *Argh!*" Forget calm. Calm was gone. Her redheaded temper overpowered all typical Carter family behavior. "You got me fired so you could get an assortment of sexual favors?"

"No, I got you fired so I could get an assortment of sexual favors *you'd* never perform for me. I never realized how much we didn't connect sexually," he said thoughtfully. "Maybe you need a therapist, Suzanne."

She tipped her head back, studied the bright blue sky and counted to ten. "I do not need a sexual therapist."

"Suzanne, seriously. I'm worried about you. You really should get help." He sounded sincerely concerned, which was totally at odds with his selfish manipulating that cost her a job. Boy, she'd really done a number on him. This post-Suzanne Tim was nothing like the sensitive, weeping Tim she'd first known.

"I've got to go, Suzanne."

"Tim—"

She heard nothing but static. *Fake* static.

"Don't you hang up on me— Damn it!" Yanking the phone from her ear, she glared at it. "I'm going to kill him," she decided and stuck another huge spoonful of ice cream in her mouth.

"But then you'd have to go directly to jail without passing Go."

Whirling around, she faced...oh, good Lord. *Ryan.* Ryan, now shirtless, and damp from what had undoubtedly been hours of hard, physical work. A fine sheen of sweat covered his chest and the light dusting of dark hair that ran from pec to glorious pec. She could feel the heat of him and suddenly could barely breathe.

Yeah, right, she needed a sexual therapist! What she needed, apparently, was a cold shower. Slowly she reached up and took the spoon out of her mouth.

"No man is worth jail," he said in the same voice he'd used on her last night, the one that made her shiver and quake from the inside out. "Even a scum like...Tim, did you say?"

Great, he'd heard it all, the entire, humiliating listing of the recent events of her pathetic life. "You were eavesdropping."

He didn't defend himself, just slowly crossed his arms over his chest and gave her that same crooked smile, accompanied with a raised brow that made her look around.

With growing horror, she realized that in her quest for phone reception, she'd backed herself right in the middle of his work zone. She was surrounded by wood rounds, chain saws and a sea of sawdust.

On either side of Ryan were two younger workers. When they caught her staring, they smiled sheepishly and turned back to their work.

Not Ryan. He just stood there looking at her. She put the spoon into the container and looked right back. From the bottom of his work boots to the top of his dark hair now decorated with wood chips, he was even more amazing than she'd remembered from last night, and she remembered him as pretty amazing.

Tim had been very good-looking, in a scholarly, professorly sort of way. Medium height, lean.

Not hard and sinewy tough, like Ryan, who looked as if he'd spent years and years honing that body with hard physical labor. She'd never really gone out with anyone like Ryan.

And didn't intend to! She was through with men, done with destroying them. She really needed to remember that.

It felt odd to be standing here like this, exchanging their first words since he'd had his arms around her the night before. When it had been dark. Raining.

Urgent.

Where she'd probably, if he'd kept on kissing her as he had, would have been willing to perform any sexual favor he wanted.

What would a sexual therapist say about that?

"You okay?" he asked quietly.

"Me? Oh, sure." She managed a laugh and hoped she didn't have a chocolate mustache. "Dandy."

"You lost your job."

"What?" Taylor came out the front door of the building, reached for Suzanne's hand. "You lost your chef position at Café Meridian?"

"Her ex got her fired," Ryan offered helpfully, still watching her very carefully. "Sounds like good riddance, wouldn't you say, Taylor?"

"Definitely." Taylor hugged Suzanne close, and while her free hand lifted and hugged back, she stared at Ryan over her shoulder. Not just because he was shirtless and magnificent, but because of the way he was looking at her.

And okay, partly because he was shirtless.

All right, mostly because he was shirtless.

But he wasn't smirking. Why wasn't he smirking? He wasn't looking at her as if she was the biggest idiot on earth. Instead, his gaze was compassionate and seemingly sincere.

She didn't buy it. Didn't want to buy it. "I'm fine," she said, and patted Taylor. "Really."

"Of course you are." Taylor pulled back and helped herself to the spoon sticking out the ice cream. "You'll just have to come up with something better, that's all." Stabbing Suzanne's spoon into the air, she said around a mouthful, "the two of us together against the world. Mmm, this is heaven. Ryan?" She offered him a bite, which he leaned over and took, opening his mouth to get it all, using his tongue to lick off the corner of his mouth.

Suzanne stared at that mouth, torn between running for the hills and demanding another kiss, right here, right now.

"Let me help you move today," Taylor said.

"But I'm jobless."

"So?"

"So...jobless equals poor. How can you possibly still want me as a tenant?"

"Do you always have ice cream available?"

"Are you kidding? Always. And I cook a lot, too."

"Thank you God," Taylor said fervently. "That's good enough for me."

"So why aren't you a caterer?" Ryan lifted his hands when both women turned to stare at him. "I'd think that would be a natural progression, from chef to caterer. And you could work for yourself. Not some flighty jerk who's going to pass off your job to your ex's new girlfriend."

Taylor turned to Suzanne, excitement lit in her eyes. "You haven't seen it yet, but the unit you're going to move into has a *huge* kitchen."

"I cater all the time," Suzanne said slowly. "As a hobby. But that's all it is, a hobby."

"So make it more," Taylor said.

Suzanne stared at her, then laughed. "It's not that easy. In fact, it's damn near impossible. Running a business just isn't my thing." Too regimented and, as her mother would attest, she just didn't do regimented.

"Hey, Ryan, *you* need a caterer," one of his laborers called out, making Suzanne realize everyone stood around listening even while they pretended not to.

The identical laborer swiped his arm across his forehead and bobbed his head. "Yeah, for our birthday party! Friday night, remember? You promised you'd have it at your place, cuz we're too young to hit the bars until next year. We need food, lots of it."

"*Lots*," agreed his twin.

Ryan stared at them both, then shook his head with a little laugh. "That's not a bad idea, actually."

When he looked at Suzanne expectantly, she let out her own little laugh. "No. No pity jobs."

"Turning down a client, Suzanne?" Ryan asked, an

unmistakable dare in his gaze as he cocked his head and made her knees weak with just one look.

Her heart pounded, and not from the dare either. Her poor body apparently hadn't gotten the memo her brain had sent, that it wasn't going to get lucky with this man.

"Don't forget, *great* kitchen," Taylor said. "And as your landlord, I give you permission to run your business out of your place."

Suzanne felt like a fool with all of them looking at her, but she was putting her foot down on this one. Opening a catering business was as bad as...as dating. A recipe for failure, and she'd failed enough. "I can't, I'm sorry."

"Would you excuse us a minute?" Taylor asked the men, and hooking an arm around Suzanne's neck, backed them up a few feet. "Are you crazy?" she whispered. "This is an excellent opportunity. A job *and* a hunk, all in the same turn."

"We swore off men," Suzanne whispered back.

"No, we swore to remain single. Nothing was said about living like a monk. Suzanne, have you seen him look at you? Do this. Do *him*. It might relax you a bit."

"Taylor!"

"Oh, it's just a job. A one-nighter at that. And hey, if I can sell off my beloved furniture to keep us in this damn building, you can make a few snacks for a party."

It burned, but Taylor was right. With a sigh, Suzanne turned back to the waiting men, then nearly swallowed her tongue at the way Ryan was looking at her, a little smile curving the lips she knew tasted better than even ice cream. "Okay."

"Okay, you'll do it?" asked Ryan's worker. "You'll cater the party?"

She looked into his hopeful eyes, and also his worker's. "I'll cater the party."

"Cool!"

Ryan just smiled, and damn if her stomach didn't quiver. "Why are you doing this?" she asked him softly.

"Doing what?"

"Being...nice."

"I'm always nice." He laughed when she merely lifted a doubtful brow. "Okay, maybe I don't like to cook."

"*Can't* you mean," offered the first worker, zipping his mouth when Ryan sent him a long look.

Hmm. So the man wasn't perfect after all. He couldn't cook. Somehow that made Suzanne feel better. A lot better.

IF SUZANNE THOUGHT about how much she'd done in just three days her head would start spinning. And seeing as she was busy hunched over a large tray, putting together the innards for egg rolls as fast as her fingers could move, now wouldn't be a good time to get overwhelmed.

She'd moved her belongings, few as they were, from the loft apartment down one flight of stairs. Taylor let her borrow some furniture so that the bigger apartment didn't seem so bare. Suzanne had scoured the South Village want-ads for a job and had blisters on her fingers from filling out applications. And because she did love it, and because she'd grown fond of eating, she agreed to several more catering jobs—as a hobby only. She and Taylor had gone outlet shopping to stock her new kitchen, which indeed, with some cleaning—aka *hours* of elbow grease—had turned out to be more than she could have hoped for.

Of course her living room was still empty except for her favorite candles here and there. And it would stay that way for a while, as she'd used her one credit card on the kitchen. But that was the least of her problems at the moment.

Ryan's workers, Rafe and Russ, she'd learned, were young, wild and wonderful. For their twentieth birthday party they vowed to eat whatever she cooked, though they'd admitted they loved Chinese food. In light of that, she'd made a huge tub of fried rice and was nearly finished the egg rolls.

And she was loving it.

As a hobby. The thought of doing this seriously as a business terrified her.

"Oh yeah, that's a girl." Russ, followed by Rafe pushed into her kitchen, their noses wriggling as they sniffed appreciatively at the scents.

"Smells heavenly," Taylor agreed, right behind them.

"Oh, man, I'll say." Russ rubbed his belly. "We're done for the day, heading home. See you there with all this food, right?"

"Right," Suzanne said, then looked at him over her shoulder. "Wait. You mean you're heading to *Ryan's* house?"

"Well, yeah. But his house used to be ours, so I still say it sometimes." Rafe reached in to steal an egg roll but Suzanne rapped him on the wrist. "His place used to be your place," she repeated as understanding dawned. "You're...brothers."

"Yep." Russ beamed. "But don't tell Ryan we told you, he doesn't like people to know we're related."

Aha! Proof positive Ryan-the-Gorgeous was indeed just a pretty face. Sure, he had a kiss that could melt bones, and sure, just a look from those dark eyes made her stupid, but inside he was petty and a big jerk. Good, because petty and jerky she could resist.

Probably.

"If everyone knew we were brothers, then the other laborers might figure out we get the best hours and more pay." Russ glanced pathetically at the egg rolls. "And if they figured that out, they'd also figure out we have less experience than some of them, and Ryan doesn't want a mutiny."

"Oh, that's so sweet," Taylor said, looking like a queen surrounded by her servants, as always dressed to the hilt. Today she wore a linen sundress with nary a wrinkle despite the fact she'd been digging through her storage unit making a list of inventory. "Isn't that sweet, Suzanne?"

Yeah, sweet.

Damn it.

"What's sweet?" Ryan wanted to know, squeezing into the kitchen with an easy smile and a shirt, thank you God, which meant maybe Suzanne had half a chance in hell on maintaining her concentration. He'd been distracting her for days, smiling at her, talking to her. Pretending to be a nice guy, which she had to admit, he seemed to have down to a science.

More reason to steer clear. She destroyed nice guys. Her aimlessness, her lack of regimentation and her Carter family ways drove men crazy, made them selfish and turned them into men who accused their exes of needing sex therapists.

Unconcerned about the danger lurking in his future, Ryan moved past the others, leaned in toward Suzanne and sniffed. "Mmm. Heaven."

She stepped aside. "It's just food."

"I meant you," he said, a smile in his eyes. "You smell like heaven."

Determined not to react even though her knees did that annoying wobble thing, she put her hands on her hips. "Why didn't you tell me I was cooking for your brothers?"

His smile didn't falter. "Would you still have taken the job?"

Damn it, probably not.

With a playful tug on her apron, he grinned. "You sure look cute in the kitchen."

He probably thought women were cute pregnant and barefoot, too. "Are you hitting on me?"

"Definitely."

She had to laugh. What else could she do? Besides, laughing hid the tremor in her voice. "Everyone out," she decided, shoving them all toward the door, ignoring the groans and moans. "Out, out, out."

"See you tonight," Ryan whispered in her ear, managing in the shuffle to stroke her jaw with his big hand. "Save me a dance."

Did he have to have such a voice on him? When he lowered it like that, all husky and suggestive, it sent shivers down her spine. Remember the vow—no men. "I don't dance."

He studied her with those sleepy, sexy eyes. "I can teach you."

"I didn't say I couldn't, I said I *don't*."

He just smiled. "We'll see."

6

AT HOME, Ryan stepped into the shower, letting the hot spray hit his body. Treeing was hard work, and damn, but he was feeling every bit of that hard work in his aching muscles.

The day would come, soon, when he'd lay down his chain saw and ax for good. Instead, he'd spend his time over a drawing table, lifting only a pencil. He'd design all day long and come home after working still refreshed.

He could...well, date even *half* the women his brothers and sister thought he did, for one. That would be fun. Light and simple.

After raising a family he was looking forward to light and simple. He hadn't thought he'd ever feel a need for any steady relationship, but he had to admit that had been before.

Before a raging stormy night, a shocking kiss and the most amazing woman had rocked his world.

Suzanne.

Maybe the problem was that he'd seen her too often since.

No, that wasn't it. He'd seen Taylor often, too, and he didn't want to make love with *her* all night long.

Maybe it was that he'd touched Suzanne. Kissed her. Held her. While she was wearing nothing but that little tank top and panties.

The picture filled out in his head, as if it had just happened, instead of having occurred five nights ago. It had been dark, with the rain and wind beating down on them. And yet she'd been like a light in the deep black of the night. He could see her rosy, erect nipples pressing at the thin material of her top, the way her panties had been sheer enough to outline the part of her he wanted to bury himself in. She had a body made for loving, all warm curvy planes, and as he soaped up in his hot shower, he gave his erection a few absentminded strokes.

That didn't help matters any so he cranked the handle to the right, letting in the cold water.

That didn't help, either.

"Ryan!" Angel yelled through the door. "I need the shower!"

"'Kay." But he went back to thinking about Suzanne. What was it about her that drew him so fiercely? She sure wasn't light and simple—which was all he'd thought he could handle right now—and she sure as hell wasn't looking at him with stars in her eyes.

But what *was* in her eyes drew him—the tough vulnerability he wanted to know more about. She had a sharp wit and a will to survive. She buried her feelings behind both.

He'd never been a sucker for vulnerability before, much preferring a woman secure and strong and self-assured, so why now, with her?

It wasn't as if she was falling at his feet, much less into his bed. He'd have to actually work at it, at her, if that's what he wanted.

And yet, he'd come to realize, that was exactly what he wanted. And he thought maybe he'd known it from the second he'd laid eyes on her.

WITH AN HOUR TO GO before everyone descended on his place in all their rowdiness, Ryan opened his door to Suzanne. She smiled, a little nervously, he thought, and vanished into his kitchen. When he followed her, he found her bustling around, talking to herself as she loaded things into his refrigerator.

"The man doesn't even have a loaf of bread," she was saying as she bent over to fit a long tray of something that smelled delicious onto the bottom shelf.

Ryan leaned against the door to better enjoy the view her black skirt afford him as it tightened very nicely over her very nice rear end.

"I would have gone food shopping yesterday," he

said, grinning when she whipped around in surprise. "But I knew you were bringing a load of food over so I didn't bother. Thank you, by the way."

"Don't thank me. You're paying dearly for it."

Had he thought her not strong or self-assured? She was sending him daggers that made him glad she stood across the room. She wore a long-sleeved white cotton shirt with a scooped neck. Though perfectly modest, it outlined her full breasts in a way that made his mouth water. The entire package made his mouth water. He'd seen her ruffled and undressed. He'd seen her casually put together in her loose and flowing sundresses. But he'd never seen her like this. Her hair was artfully piled on top of her head with a pretty beaded clip, though he had a feeling that with one tug of his fingers, the entire glorious mass would fall. Already long wavy tendrils were hanging in her face, which had flushed prettily.

Because of him? Testing that theory, he pushed away from the wall and moved close, cocking his head when she backed up a step and hit the counter.

Hmm. Interesting.

She put her hands behind her to grip the counter, which suited him perfectly because it thrust out her upper body very nicely. Specifically, her breasts.

"You're crowding me," she said.

"Am I?" Stepping even closer, he put his hands

over hers on the tile and promptly got lost in the depths of her shimmering eyes, which displayed...nerves? "You're...not afraid of me."

"Of course not."

"But I make you nervous."

"Don't be ridiculous—" She caught his lifted brow and let out a pent-up breath that blew a piece of hair off her face at the same time. "Okay, maybe just a little nervous, but only when you look at me like...like *that*."

"Like what?"

"Like you're dying of thirst and I'm a long, cold drink of water."

He decided he liked that, a lot more than he should. "What, exactly, are you saying?" he asked in a perverted need to hear her spell it out.

"I'm saying you fry my brain cells at an alarming rate. Clear enough?"

"Crystal." And he was quite certain it shouldn't arouse him.

He wanted to scoop her up and lose himself in her. How was it she was so completely irresistible to him after only days?

"I'm busy," she said, clearly having not decided, as he had, that this attraction was a good thing.

Oh, yeah, he had a lot of convincing to do. He stroked his hands up her arms and felt her shiver.

"Go away and let me work," she said, a little less forcefully. "Before I decide to charge you more for the conversation."

"We're not talking." It took nothing to dip his head and inhale the scent lingering on the skin just beneath her ear. Shampoo and soap only, he thought breathing in deeply. No fancy perfumes for this woman. He loved that. "I fry your brain cells? Really?"

With another little shiver, goose bumps appeared on her skin, and proved he wasn't alone in this attraction.

Good, because he couldn't tear himself away.

"You know you do," she whispered, gasping when he connected his mouth with the creamy skin of her throat.

She put her hands to his chest, probably to shove him away, but before she could, he slid his hands over hers, holding them against his chest because he liked the feel of them there.

"I said you fried my brain cells." She swallowed hard, staring at her hands on him. "Not that I liked it."

"If you don't, why are you letting me touch you?"

She stared at him. Then laughed. "I...don't know."

"Are you going to deny you like my touch?"

"Ryan—"

He slid one of his hands up her soft throat to cup her jaw. "We never talked about that night, Suzanne. About what happened between us."

"We were cold and wet. It was dark, and I was scared. We kissed. The end."

"Not the end."

"Okay, you're right. You saved my life. Thank you. From the bottom of my heart, thank you. *Now* it's the end."

Slowly he shook his head while his thumb stroked her jaw, stopping to outline her full lower lip, which trembled and fell open. "Something happened between us," he said quietly. "You know it."

She licked her lips, and a vision of him exploring her mouth with his tongue entered his head and wouldn't go away.

"This is such a bad idea. I've given up men, you know."

It was his turn to stare at her, then laugh.

"I have. Hey, it's for *your* sake."

He thought about that, and the sudden nervous look that appeared in her eyes despite the smile on her lips. "I'm not like him, Suzanne," he said very softly. "Your ex-fiancé."

"Which one?" Holding up a hand when he winced at her, she let out a low laugh. "Yeah. There were three. I ruined them all."

"I doubt that."

"No, it's true. I'm on a roll. You should run. Really."

"Sounds like you only tried the idiots of my gender."

"I've tried more than my fair share," she admitted. "And I've failed at keeping anyone happy. Badly. I consider myself an expert at them. Failed relationships, that is. But to be fair, I inherited the gift from my father, who was married and divorced six times before he met my mom. I think he sticks with her because she'd kill him if he divorced her, so really, that marriage doesn't count—"

"Suzanne." He had no idea why she'd gotten to him so hard, so fast, but his entire heart, locked off to others for so long, squeezed for her. "First, I keep myself happy, I don't rely on a woman to do that, ever. No man should. And second—"

"No. No second," she said quickly.

"And second, I want you. More than I've ever wanted another woman."

He saw in her eyes the wanting in return, before she covered her face. "Oh my God, it's only been a few days!"

"Five. A lifetime."

"I can't believe I'm doing this. Why aren't you running? You should be running. Seriously, I drive men crazy."

"Suzanne." He had to laugh, and pulled her hands from her face. "Believe me, I'd love to run, but it's too late for me."

"No. Oh, Ryan, no, don't say it. It's never too late." She opened those green, green eyes, and in them was a pleading he couldn't resist. "I'm already so nervous about the food that I can barely function. Please, you have to go."

"The food is going to be a huge hit." Hell, she could have served chips and dip and they'd all be thrilled, but he figured she didn't need to hear that right now. "Let me help you get ready."

"Okay, yes." She put her hands on his shoulders and shoved him toward the door. "Help me by getting out."

RYAN WAS RIGHT, the food was a huge hit. Suzanne marveled over that a few hours later when all but a few bites of it had vanished.

The crowd was a young one, and given the decibel level of voices and music in the place, they were having a great time.

She was having a great time. Ryan's brothers were so cute, it was hard not to. They clearly worshipped Ryan, regaling her with stories about the way he'd kept them together, his job, his...what had they called it? His "chick magnetism."

A magnetism she could resist, she told herself.

Yeah, maybe if she was dead.

Russ and Rafe worked the rooms, keeping everyone in smiles, especially the women, which made Suzanne think they just might be more like Ryan than they knew.

And when they turned down the lights and shoved the furniture back to open the place up for dancing, Suzanne whirled back to vanish into the kitchen.

And came face-to-face with Ryan. He wore khakis tonight, and a plain soft-looking white shirt that showed off his sun-bronzed skin and crooked smile. "Where's the fire?" he asked.

"Um..."

Before she could come up with a suitable excuse, he took her hand and led her onto the hardwood floor of his darkened living room.

"What are you doing?" she asked in a panicked whisper, pulling back uselessly against his unyielding grip.

"Dancing." Right in the middle of everyone, he pulled her into his arms.

No one paid them the slightest bit of attention, so unless she wanted to create a scene, she didn't seem to have a choice but to—ohmigod—dance.

"Relax," he whispered into her ear when she held herself stiffly to minimize their body contact. He ran his big hands down her spine. "This is supposed to be fun."

"I don't really consider dancing fun."

"Don't you know how to dance?"

She looked up into his eyes. "I used to dance on top of tables. My second fiancé got me the job."

"Yes, well, we've already established what I think of the men in your past."

"It...doesn't bother you?"

"That you danced on tables for what probably was damn good money? Not if you enjoyed it."

"No, that I've been engaged so many times and ruined so many good men."

"I doubt *you* ruined anyone, Suzanne."

She stared at him. "That's not how the story goes."

"*Did* you really fail anyone?" he asked softly. "And before you answer, think about it. Did you lie, steal or cheat anyone? Did you do anything other than be who you are, which is a smart, funny, beautiful, compassionate, *amazing* woman?"

She swallowed. "You...scare me."

"Good. You scare me back. Now you've stopped dancing. Can't have that. Here, ease up against me a bit, that's right, like that."

Oh God. Their bodies brushed together, hers doing

just as he said, easing up against him. Pleasure suffused her entire being, blooming from all the contact points, of which there were many.

She was well aware of how easy it would be to take that pleasure. To give some back. They could spend the night together. Pressed against him as she was, she could feel he was more than ready and able and willing.

But at what cost? She couldn't do this again. She just couldn't. Plus, to add to her growing fears, this didn't feel like any of the other relationships she'd had, this felt...deeper. In less than a week, it felt like more. Oh, God.

The music slowed, and so did Ryan. "Nice, huh?" His low voice was soft by her ear, his hands holding her close, but she had the feeling she'd be this close even without his encouragement, as her body seemed to have a mind of its own.

When he swayed, she swayed, when he turned, she turned. For a man who worked outside with his hands all day long, he was amazingly sensual. Extraordinarily erotic. And being held against him, swaying, dipping, she became those things, too. She was surrounded by him—by his touch, his voice— and nothing in her experience had ever felt so good, so very good. In his arms, her resolve to resist him at all costs faded away to nothing. Less than nothing. In fact, if he scooped her up against him and carried her off to his bed, she'd probably beg him to hurry.

Then they shifted even closer so that the tips of her breasts slid against his chest. Her hips pressed to his, allowing her to feel his hard belly, his hard thighs and the most interesting hard bulge between them. Lifting her gaze, she saw the heat and desire smoldering in his, just waiting for her to acknowledge it.

"You do that to me," he murmured.

She trembled and forgot why she was holding back.

"Do I do that to you, too, Suzanne? Make you hot? Make you feel like you could just...spontaneously combust?"

"I..." The words backed up in her throat when his gaze dipped to the scooped neckline of her shirt. The plump curves of her breasts just barely showed. Modest. She'd meant for it to be so. But he pulled back an inch, just enough so that she could see the clear, defined outline of her nipples pressing so desperately against the material of her shirt.

"Yes," she whispered, admitting the truth he could see. "You...do that to me."

"Are you wet, too?" he asked, very softly near her ear. "Are you wet for me?"

A helpless whimper escaped her when he pulled her close again, swaying lightly to the music.

Good thing *he* could still dance. Her pulse had long ago skyrocketed. Everywhere they touched sent an electrical current through her body, pooling at the spot between her legs. Breathing unevenly, she swallowed hard, but her heart still threatened to burst right out of her chest.

If Ryan noticed, he gave no sign, merely dipped his head a little and gently slid his jaw to hers. The unexpected tenderness of that and the way he guided her around the living room with such ease made her feel almost sorry she was never going to try again, that she'd never experience love the way she knew it must exist.

Then the music ended, and he slowly pulled back, releasing her. She nearly cried. *More, please more,* she wanted to plead, and bit her tongue instead. A little pain now would save her later, she told herself.

But there, in the dark, they stood. She could feel him looking at her. She couldn't imagine what he was thinking. Then the music started back up and she felt his fingers once again entwine with hers. They were warm and slightly rough from all the hard work he did every day. "One more," he said, and when she hesitated a heartbeat too long, he drew her back against him.

A small sound of pure pleasure escaped her at the feel of his long, hard body once again against hers.

Who would have believed a dance could be so sensual, so...overwhelming?

Dipping his head so that he could see into her eyes, he held her gaze, holding her to him as if maybe he didn't want to let her go either.

Tim had never held her like this, as if she was a beautiful creature, as if he'd die if she moved away.

No one had.

It was terribly seductive, and terribly revealing. She was going to cave if she wasn't careful! God, what could she do? Calculate complicated recipes in her head? Remember she was essentially jobless?

She still wanted him with a desperation that scared her spitless. This time when the music ended, she pulled back. "I...have to clean up."

"Don't go."

"Have to," she whispered, and at his expression— so completely frustrated and ardent at the same time—she ran into the kitchen, where she went straight to the sink, turned on the cold water, and splashed her face until reason returned.

Then, and only then, did she clean up the kitchen. As soon as she finished, she let herself out the back door into the dark night. She raced home and fell into bed, reaching beneath her pillow for the book of jokes her father had given her when her heart had first been broken. She'd been twelve, and Steven Mac-

Kenzie had publicly dumped her at second recess. It had been her first lesson at laughing in the face of pain and ever since, when she'd been down, she'd read the book to put herself to sleep.

But tonight, no jokes, no matter how familiar and comforting, helped.

7

THE NEXT AFTERNOON Suzanne and Taylor sat on Taylor's big bed, eating ice cream right out of the container. "It was horrible," Suzanne said.

"I don't know how you can say that. I've tried it myself."

"Really? Did you feel like your heart was going to just leap right out of your chest?"

"No, Chinese food doesn't do that to me. But Mexican does."

"Not the food!" Suzanne shook her head and laughed. "I'm talking about the slow dancing!"

"Well." Even Taylor's eyes smiled. "Well, well."

"And what does that mean?"

"It means I find it very interesting that a man you claim to feel nothing for can make your heart go all pitter-pattery when he holds you against him."

Obviously Taylor had never been held against the likes of Ryan Alondo. And until last night, Suzanne hadn't either. She'd never experienced such a true, desperate need for a man in her life. She'd been so frantic she would have given up breathing to have him.

"And yet you kept slow dancing," Taylor pointed out.

"Well..." Remembering how heavenly it had felt being held tight to his hard, warm body, Suzanne sighed. "Yeah."

"But in the end, you somehow managed to walk away without jumping his bones."

"Not walk," Suzanne corrected. "Run. I ran like hell was nipping at my heels."

"I don't know about hell, honey, but I'd certainly call him sin personified."

They both looked out the window—where Sin Personified was working a story below. Ryan stood on a large round of wood, balanced on the balls of his feet. His shirt clung to him, damp with exertion, which only further defined a body she knew could made a grown woman cry, but that's not what caught her attention now. He was wielding a huge ax with the rhythm of a machine, his arms, his chest, his legs all working in perfect unison.

Suzanne had tried to pick up one of those axes the other day. She'd barely been able to get it off the ground, much less fling it with deadly precision over her head time and time again.

"God, he's gorgeous." Taylor slid another bite of

ice cream into her mouth. "Mmm. Sort of rugged and earthy, you know? With just the slightest bit of edge and danger mixed in. I mean, look at him." She sucked on her spoon with a dreamy look on her exquisite face. "I bet he's an exceptional lover."

Oh yeah, he would be. With those hands? Long and lean and work-roughened. They were dark from the sun, warm, and Suzanne could almost feel them stroking over her much paler skin... Her legs tightened, halfway to orgasm just thinking about it, and she had to laugh. "I'm sure he's far too experienced for me."

Taylor lifted a worldly brow. "Are you saying our tree guy gets around?"

"His brothers told me he's a chick magnet." She rolled her eyes. "Their words, not mine."

Her landlord pursed her lips and fanned herself. "A man who knows what he's doing. Yummy."

Yummy was right, and Suzanne was starting to perspire with all the images running wild in her head. "Can we talk about something else?"

"Sure. How about this?" Sitting Indian-style on her bed, Taylor spread out a set of blue prints and a thick file. "Bids. I need an architect, an engineer and a contractor, and that's just to start. I've seen three of each so far. My God, do you have any idea how much these people charge?"

"A lot?"

"More than an arm and a leg, let me tell you. But I figure if I sell off the antiques, I can do this, assuming, of course, that I never need to eat or heat the place again."

"No problem," Suzanne said. "This is Southern California, we'll live without heating. As for the eating part, I have two more catering jobs coming up. A promotion party and a housewarming get-together."

"Good for you! You should toss the want ads I see you scanning every day and go for it."

"Oh, no. Catering's just a hobby. But with the few odd jobs here and there, I can keep us fed." Suzanne leaned over the blue prints, which she had no idea how to read, looking up when she felt Taylor go utterly still. "What's the matter?"

Taylor looked stunned. "You...you just said you'd feed me."

"Yeah, like your skinny little butt needs much."

"But...that's the sweetest thing anyone ever said to me." Her smile a bit watery now, she held out her spoon in a cheers. "To not needing heating this year."

Suzanne toasted her right back. "To a steady job to keep us in ice cream."

"To lots of sexy guys working on this place," Taylor said and grinned. "Might as well get some good scenery out of the deal."

"And last but not least..." Suzanne firmly kept her gaze off the window and the sexiest shirtless guy in the entire world as she lifted her spoon in another toast. "To remaining single."

"To remaining single," Taylor agreed. "Which does *not* preclude having sex when available—under responsible conditions, of course."

Of course. And that, unfortunately, was the problem.

She couldn't stop thinking about sex, responsible or otherwise.

THE NEXT EVENING, Suzanne slaved away in her kitchen, cooking like a fiend for the upcoming promotion party.

As always, she had vanilla candles lit, both for a relaxing aid, and also because she loved the flickering glow and scent.

Taylor sat on the counter, stuffing her face as fast as Suzanne stuffed the giant mushrooms. "I'm going to need another tenant," she said around a full bite. "Soon as I get the wall in the loft fixed. And God save us from deadbeats."

"I'll toast to that." They lifted their lemonade, then each chased it with a stuffed mushroom.

"Good God, can you cook." Taylor moaned over another bite. "Where did you learn? Your mom?"

Suzanne laughed. "My mom's idea of cooking is pressing a button on the microwave. What I do baffles her. She's a teacher, and has always wanted me to be noble and do the same."

Taylor shuddered. "Deal with kids? Just kill me now."

Suzanne stopped stuffing mushrooms and smiled. "That's what I like most about you. You'd never let someone tell you who and what to be."

"You wouldn't either."

"Ah, but you're wrong there." Stalling, Suzanne flipped on the kitchen light, as the sun had nearly set. Out her window came the glow of halogen lights from Ryan's crew, who were still working. "Up until very recently I did exactly that, let people tell me what to do. My mother wanted me to teach, so I taught. Kindergarten. Wiped running noses all day long."

Taylor shuddered again.

"Then my first fiancé wanted me to be a nurse, but I didn't have the right education, so I became a medical assistant instead."

"Ugh."

"No kidding. The day a nurse handed me a bed pan, I walked."

Taylor laughed, then slapped a hand over her mouth. "I'm sorry."

"Don't be, it gets worse. My next fiancé thought I should be an exotic dancer. And since that horrified my mother, it was actually a bonus for a while—kind of payback for the runny noses."

Taylor's eyes were shining with sympathy and laughter. "You didn't."

"I so did."

"Well, you have the body for it."

"The men certainly thought so, but dancing on tables wasn't my thing." The teaching had given her momentary prestige, the medical profession a sense of purpose. But all the dancing had gotten her was good cash tips. She'd been left feeling...aimless. Until the cooking gig. "My last fiancé—"

"The crybaby jerk?"

"Right. The crybaby jerk. He got me started on the chef thing. Which is more than I can say for anyone else in my life."

"What happened to them all?"

"The fiancés?" Suzanne lifted a shoulder. "I destroyed whatever they felt for me. One by one."

"I doubt that you did that single-handedly."

"I'm bad at love, Taylor. Just ask any of them. I'm aimless and not serious enough. I hurt each of them and it didn't take that long either."

"Love sucks," Taylor said with a finality that told Suzanne she knew of what she spoke. Suzanne opened her mouth to ask about it but glanced at a movement by the door.

Ryan stood there, his big body filling the doorway. Given his intense eyes and the lack of his usual smile, she'd guess he'd heard everything. Despite that, his physical presence captured her gaze and wouldn't let it go.

Just looking at him made her feel a little weak, a little needy, when she hated both. Could he understand, really understand, that no matter how they nearly exploded every time they simply got within touching distance, she couldn't give in?

She wouldn't hurt another soul.

"I don't intend to ruin another man," she said to Taylor, never taking her eyes off Ryan.

"Well, who needs men anyway?" Taylor turned to Ryan and bit her lower lip, a mischievous smile slowly curving her lips. "Though I have to say, they do have their occasional uses. The recreational sport of sex, for instance. What do you think, Suzanne?"

Ryan, the tall, big, sexy jerk, simply smiled. "Yes, Suzanne," he said ever so politely while his eyes smoldered. "What do you think?"

"That I've given *you* enough stuffed mushrooms," Suzanne muttered, grabbing the tray from Taylor. On second thought, she snatched the tall glass of lemonade from her as well.

Taylor only laughed, then hopped off the counter. Tossing back her mane of blond hair, she kissed Suzanne on the cheek. "Don't get all snippy now. I was just trying to prove a point."

"Which would be?"

"That having wild monkey sex with a man is *not* the same thing as giving up your life for one." Leaning forward she said in a mock whisper, "In other words, *go for it.*" Straightening, she winked at Ryan. "See you later." Waving perfectly manicured fingernails, she walked right out of the kitchen.

Leaving Ryan alone with the woman he couldn't seem to get enough of.

"I meant what I said," Suzanne said to him, turning her back, busying her hands with something in a bowl. "I don't need a man."

Only a few weeks ago, Ryan would have said he didn't need a woman, either. But there was a churning in his gut when he looked at her that he'd never experienced before, a need. An insatiable hunger.

Oh yeah, he needed a woman. He needed *her*.

"I don't need *anyone*," she added into the silence.

"So you've said." Moving in close, he put his hands on her hips. He liked putting his hands on her, and it was time she knew it. He peeked over her shoulder into the bowl, and his poor, neglected stomach growled. "What's cooking?"

She sighed, but didn't move away.

Progress, he decided.

"You're hungry," she said with another sigh. "Of course you are, you worked like a dog today. Have a seat and I'll—"

The lights flickered once and went out.

Suzanne gasped, and Ryan gently squeezed his fingers on her hips, touched beyond belief that she'd noticed him working so hard, that in spite of whatever complicated feelings she had, she'd stop everything to see him fed. "You actually made me forget what I came to tell you," he said. "The electricity is going off for a bit, just while Rafe cuts down a branch too close to the electrical lines. We'd do it tomorrow, but there's supposed to be a Santa Ana wind coming through. It's dangerous to wait."

She whirled to face him, and he caught her scent, the sweet, clean scent that tickled him in his dreams. A strand of her hair clung to his jaw and he held still so that it stayed there.

"But I have to finish cooking. I need electricity to finish."

"It won't be long. You still have the candlelight." Which was meager at best, since there were only three little ones left burning. He'd left his hands on her hips, and fought the urge to glide them over her entire body.

"W-what am I supposed to do in the meantime?"

Hell if that wasn't a loaded question. "We could talk."

"It was just a dance," she said defensively, referring to the party.

"Like the kiss was just a kiss?"

"Yes." But her breath caught, and in the glow of the candlelight, he looked into her unsure face.

Snagged by that, and the way she felt in his hands, he shifted closer, and when she let out a little murmur of helpless pleasure at the feel of him, he pressed closer still. "Suzanne." She thought herself some kind of man destroyer, but the truth as he saw it was, *she'd* been hurt. She didn't trust easily. She wasn't someone to toy with. He knew this, just as he knew he should walk away. But he'd already decided he wouldn't do that.

Instead, he glided his hands up her arms, over her soft throat, to her face, which he cupped, wishing he could see her more clearly. "Suzanne...what's happening here?"

"I...don't know what you mean."

His hips bumped hers, she let out that helpless hum again, and this time he groaned. "You feel it. I know you do."

"It's just..." Her breathing quickened, and she put her hands on his shoulders, gripping hard, as if she needed the balance. "It's just what Taylor said. A healthy need for recreational sex."

"So if we had sex, right here, right now, you're saying the need between us would vanish?"

He didn't need any light to know she stood there with her mouth open, and he let out a groaning laugh, putting his forehead to hers. "Okay, let's find you a flashlight or more candles so I can get the hell out of here before I take advantage of your unbelievably arousing silence."

"No one takes advantage of me." As if to prove that statement, she slid her hands into his hair and fisted them, tugging him closer. Her warm breath brushed his cheek, her long, loose hair slid over his arm.

He nearly inhaled her. God, he could eat her up.

"Come to think of it," she murmured. "*I've* never taken advantage of anyone either. Funny, because I've always wanted to." She rocked against him. "Think I could take advantage of you, Ryan?"

He went instantly hard, and he opened his mouth to offer himself as a sacrifice when she covered his mouth with hers.

Just like before, instantaneous combustion, and oh man, the feel of her in his hands, against him, letting out that rough little sound in the back of her throat...

Her fingers tightened in his hair, as if she was

afraid he'd pull away. Not a chance, he would have told her, if her tongue hadn't been dancing with his. He wouldn't have pulled away even if he was suffocating.

Suzanne wasn't suffocating, she was drowning, in pleasure. She had the cold counter at her back and a hard Ryan at her front, and yet she'd never felt so hot in her life. The lack of light only lent to the intimacy somehow, and that brought her back enough to break away to say on a gasping breath, "This is just what we said, no more, no less."

"Sex."

"*Just* sex. And when we're done..."

"We're done," he finished.

Was she imagining things or did he sound sceptical, as though he didn't believe it?

"Right." She was practically panting now, and so was he. "Itch scratched," she added.

"Right."

"Promise?" She held his head, squinted through the dark to see his gaze.

"Suzanne..."

"No, you have to promise. You have to because..." She hesitated, then said on a shaky breath, "because I've never had 'just sex' before."

He looked shocked, Suzanne thought, very shocked.

"Never?"

"Never," she admitted. "I want to have sex without getting engaged, Ryan."

He hesitated, damn him. "No," she said fiercely. "Don't hesitate."

"I feel something for you, Suzanne, something I don't understand yet and I won't make a promise I can't be sure I can keep."

"You have to," she said, and heard her own desperation.

"What if more than just sex is better?"

"No. Promise, Ryan. Please."

For the longest moment, he just looked at her, her dark and beautiful tree man.

"Ryan? Promise me."

Night had fallen around them, so that without the electricity, there was little but candlelight and the faint glow from the building across the street. The sound of the wind outside the window felt rhythmic, hypnotic, and so did the feel of Ryan engulfing her in his embrace.

When he groaned and pulled her even closer, she melted against him. And some of the odd emptiness she'd been feeling faded. They could do this and be done with it. Get on with their lives. And afterwards, this inexplicable need for each other would just go away.

No entanglements.

No broken hearts.

That made this okay, didn't it? She wouldn't hurt him, because this was all they'd have.

She wanted to believe that, oh, how she wanted to believe, because his mouth was so firm, and so deliciously demanding, she couldn't help but sink back into the mindlessness of it, needing the mindlessness of it.

"Suzanne..." Just beneath her ear, he sucked on a patch of skin, and made her knees weak. "I love the way you hold onto me when I touch you."

She was. She was clinging to him as if he were her entire life, and instead of jerking away at the knowledge, she wrapped her arms around his neck and arched to him.

"Oh yeah, like that," he said on a low growl. "Yeah, like that." He kissed her again—longer, wetter, deeper. He had a wonderful mouth, a make-her-forget-everything mouth, and he knew just what to do with it to make her wild.

"Suzanne?"

No. No talking. Trying to tell him, she arched her body to his. Had Tim said she needed a sexual therapist? Was he insane? She needed a hose to put out the fire!

"Stop me now if you're going to," Ryan said in a

low growl as he ran openmouthed kisses down her throat.

Not a chance. Instead she leaned in and bit his lower lip, making him groan, making him lift her against him so that her feet dangled as he devoured her mouth with his.

While they gobbled each other up, she took her hands on a tour over his amazing arms, his wide shoulders, feeling her insides rev up because he turned her on so much. Thank God his hesitation had pretty much walked. It might return in the light of day but she didn't want to face that now, she didn't want to face anything but this. And now that her eyes had adjusted to the dark, she could really see him, the way he was looking at her, and for the first time she understood true lust and the power of it.

He sat her on the counter, then held her head for a long, hungry kiss before making his way down her neck, all the while sliding his hands over her thighs to her knees, urging them open so he could step between them, press up against her.

He was hard, so gloriously hard, her breath caught.

"Mmm, love that sound," he murmured, making her sigh again, against his throat, a sigh that bubbled up into her throat, changing into a moan when he cupped her breasts. Her sundress had buttons down the front to her belly, four of them. She knew this because, catching her gaze in his hot one, he popped them open. One. At. A. Time.

Then he looked down at her, and slowly pushed the material off her shoulders. With one finger he traced the edging of her bra, from one side to the other. Her nipples had long ago beaded to two tight little tips, but she couldn't believe how erotic it was to sit there, spread open for him, and watch him watch her while he touched her.

He opened the front hook on her bra and peeled that material away, too, letting out a deep heartfelt groan at the sight revealed. Cupping her in his hands, he used his thumbs to trace the underside of the heavy curves, lightly, so lightly.

Her nipples went even harder. Her hips involuntarily thrust upward.

Then he danced his fingers over her nipples, making her let out a horribly needy sound from deep in her throat. "Ryan..."

"I know." Bending his head, he pulled a hard tip into his mouth, using first his tongue, then his teeth on her, until she made the sound again.

By the time he drew her in deep and sucked, she was practically sobbing his name. Barely remembering she'd started this, that *she* was supposedly taking advantage of *him*, she wrapped her legs around his waist and pressed against that most interesting hard bulge there.

He answered by popping her breast free, then staring down at the wet nipple while tracing it with his thumb. "You're so soft. So perfect." While he said this, he bunched up her dress to her waist, not difficult since it was lightweight and loose and gauzy.

It gave her a bad moment, wondering if he preferred skinny women, and she tried to suck in her stomach, but he let out such a genuine sigh at the sight of her, she instantly forgot about her imperfections.

His hands slid inside the back of her panties, cupping her bottom, pressing her even closer so that she could feel exactly what this little interlude had done to him.

Just thinking about it, feeling him rock against the neediest part of her body, made her weak and trembly. She was close, so very unbelievably close, and he'd hardly touched her. But her toes were already curling, and she had to, *had* to have more. Wrapping her arms around his neck, she bit his lower lip and said in a shaky voice she hardly recognized as her own. "*Please*, Ryan."

"Whatever you want," he promised hoarsely.

And then the lights came on.

8

ONCE AGAIN Ryan stood in his shower, trying to relieve some tension. This time it was sexual tension.

It had been over a week since he'd first set eyes on Suzanne. He had no idea how long a guy could walk around with an erection without having his parts fall off, but he was thinking it couldn't be too much longer.

Damn, his brothers had bad timing, getting the electricity back on just as he'd gotten his hands inside Suzanne's panties, and a glorious breast in his mouth.

Just one more minute, one more, and he'd have been buried deep in her sweet, hot body.

Instead, the lights had blared on, jarring them both. Suzanne had jerked, staring at him wide- and wild-eyed.

Wanting to soothe, wanting to get back to that mindless pleasure they'd shared, Ryan had leaned in, only to have her slap a hand to his chest and shake her head.

Dress bunched around her waist and tugged off her shoulders, she'd dragged in a shuddering breath.

Her nipples had been tight, and wet from his mouth. Her panties, stretched over her mound and bared to him by her opened legs, had been wet, too, and just thinking about it made him hard all over again.

"Ryan?" Angel pounded on his bathroom door.

In typical brotherly fashion, he cranked the hot water back up and ignored her.

"I've got dinner cooking for you, okay?"

Ah, hell. He turned off the water.

"And don't forget, that woman Rafe set you up with? The...'hot chick' I think he said? Anyway, she called just now to say she'd pick you up. Gotta run now, late for class. Bye!"

"What? *Wait!*" Wrapping a towel around his hips he opened the bathroom door just in time to hear the front door slam. "Angel?"

Of course she didn't come back, it was her mission in life to screw with his.

But...what woman? Vaguely he remembered Rafe telling him he'd met someone who'd be "perfect" for him, but having heard that too many times to count, he'd just nodded and ignored him.

It was his job as big brother to ignore his siblings when they talked too much.

But now he had a bad feeling he'd ignored something important. If he had some hot date, he'd like to know about it.

The Harlequin Reader Service® — Here's how it works:

If offer card is missing write to: Harlequin Reader Service, 3010 Walden Ave., P.O. Box 1867, Buffalo NY 14240-1867

NO POSTAGE
NECESSARY
IF MAILED
IN THE
UNITED STATES

BUSINESS REPLY MAIL
FIRST-CLASS MAIL   PERMIT NO. 717-003   BUFFALO, NY

POSTAGE WILL BE PAID BY ADDRESSEE

HARLEQUIN READER SERVICE
3010 WALDEN AVE
PO BOX 1867
BUFFALO NY 14240-9952

GET FREE BOOKS and a FREE GIFT WHEN YOU PLAY THE...

Lucky 7

SLOT MACHINE GAME!

Just scratch off the silver box with a coin. Then check below to see the gifts you get!

YES! I have scratched off the silver box. Please send me the 2 free Harlequin Temptation® books and gift for which I qualify. I understand I am under no obligation to purchase any books, as explained on the back of this card.

342 HDL DRRP

142 HDL DRR5
(H-T-01/03)

FIRST NAME	LAST NAME

ADDRESS

APT.#	CITY

STATE/PROV.	ZIP/POSTAL CODE

7	7	7	**Worth TWO FREE BOOKS plus a BONUS Mystery Gift!**
🍒	🍒	🍒	**Worth TWO FREE BOOKS!**
♣	♣	♣	**Worth ONE FREE BOOK!**
🔔	🔔	🍒	**TRY AGAIN!**

Visit us online at www.eHarlequin.com

Offer limited to one per household and not valid to current Harlequin Temptation® subscribers. All orders subject to approval.

DETACH AND MAIL CARD TODAY!

But good, bad or "perfect," no woman came to his door that night.

LATE THE NEXT AFTERNOON, Suzanne sat on the front steps of Taylor's building, watching life go by, pretending not to stare at Ryan, once again shirtless and hard at work.

He was nearly finished with the trees.

Soon he'd go off to the next job, wherever that might be, and she was fine with that. More than fine.

So why, then, did her heart squeeze just watching him work?

Simple, pure, unadulterated physical reaction to a gorgeous man, she decided, a man intense and sweaty and hard at work. There was nothing sexier than that.

But she was becoming deathly afraid that much of it had nothing to do with sex, or even lust.

With a sigh, she straightened the newspaper in her hands with a little shake and buried her nose in the want ads. A catering job here and there wasn't good enough. She needed her regimentation.

Just ask her mother.

With another sigh, she circled a chef position at a restaurant only a few blocks over, then looked up as a shadow fell over her.

"Hey," said the voice that never failed to make her

stomach flip-flop. Ryan's long, hard body stood right in front of her, so that her head was perfectly level with the juncture at the top of his thighs, and the most fascinating spot between them—

"Whatcha doing?"

She jerked her gaze back to the paper. "Reading."

"The want ads?"

"Funny thing, how attracted I am to having a positive balance in my bank account."

A finger hooked into the paper, pulled it down, exposing a curious, interested, gorgeously rumpled Ryan. What was it about a sweaty man?

"What about the catering gig?" he asked.

She was careful to keep her gaze averted. "It's just a hobby."

"It's more than that."

"No, really it's just a hobby. Sure I've had more contacts and jobs lately, but I'm not into my own business." A tad too much regimentation there. "It's a good hobby." She circled another chef ad. The only other one in the paper.

"Just don't give up," he said with a fierceness that surprised her into looking up past his long, long legs and what lay between, all the way up to his deeply passionate expression.

"I won't," she said with some surprise. Funny how

the thought of *not* doing her catering didn't sit well. "I wouldn't."

"Good." He pulled on his shirt. Uncapping a water bottle, he sat at her side, leaned back on one elbow and tipped back his head to drink.

His Adam's apple, such an utterly male thing, bobbed with each swallow. His light blue T-shirt clung to his damp, overworked body. His powerful denim-clad legs were stretched out in front of him, his booted feet crossed in utter relaxation.

A long sigh escaped him as he finished off the water, wiping his mouth with the back of his hand. "That's good."

What was good was how he looked. She wanted to lick the last drop off his bottom lip. *Down, girl.* "You're done for the day?"

"Yes, ma'am. Nearly done period. Just a couple of hours tomorrow and that's it."

Yeah, that's about what she figured. "What about the trees in the back?"

"Why?" He turned his head to face her. "You going to miss me?"

Only every living second. "Of course not."

"Right." He turned forward again, his face unreadable. "And we trimmed those already."

"Oh. You're...um, good at what you do."

He looked at her from beneath half-closed, sleepy,

sexy eyes, and she realized how her words had sounded. "I meant, the trees," she said quickly. "You're good at the trees."

His expression was silent and searching, his big body so close the yearning nearly overtook her.

"I've been doing it for a long time," he finally said. "That's all."

There was a weariness in his voice now that made her hesitate.

Don't ask.

Don't dig.

It doesn't concern you. *He* doesn't concern you. "Is something the matter?"

He looked surprised at the question, and that tugged at her, too. He was surrounded by people, she knew that now. People who depended on him. His brothers. His sister. His laborers.

But who did *he* depend on?

"I'm just tired of trees," he admitted, letting out that melting crooked smile while he stretched his long body and groaned. "My body is tired of trees. I'll be glad when..."

Though she waited, he didn't finish. He just closed his mouth, put his sunglasses back over his eyes and tilted up his face to the sinking sun.

"Ryan? You'll be glad when...what?"

A honk from the street startled them both. At the

curb sat a bright red Miata. A woman got out, a brunette with legs from here to New York.

Ryan knew this because she wore a leather miniskirt that showed them off, topped by heels that screamed do me! Her top was leather too, but didn't quite meet the skirt, exhibiting a sparkling stud in her quite exposed belly button.

But what confused Ryan was the way she beelined right toward *him*, her very red lips in a welcoming smile that he didn't understand.

Him? She was smiling at him?

He craned his neck and checked behind him to make sure, but the only people on the steps were himself and Suzanne.

"Ryan?" Long Legs held out her slim hand, which he automatically took. "I'm Allene." She smiled expectantly, as if waiting for him to slap his forehead and say, "Of course. *Allene.*"

Allene. Allene. Who the hell was Allene and why was she looking at him like that, as if she'd like to gobble him up in one bite? He looked at Suzanne, who was still looking at Allene.

He came to his feet as the woman said, "I know we arranged for me to pick you up at home, but I heard you were working down here, and I drive right by every day, so I thought..." She trailed off and smiled again.

Suddenly Angel's message the other night made sense. Everything clicked into place.

His brother.

This was the "hot chick" Rafe had set him up with, without permission, and while she was definitely hot and definitely a chick, he didn't want... Ah, hell.

Suzanne was staring at him.

Allene was staring at him.

And Ryan was going to kill his meddling younger brother. Russ wouldn't mind being without his twin—Rafe was a pain in all their asses. He'd be doing the family a favor. "I'm sorry, there's been a mistake. My brother..."

"Oh, for Pete's sake, just go with her." This from Suzanne, who stood up and dusted off her hands. "Have fun."

"Suz—"

"'Night!" And she was gone, the door to the building shut in his face. Shut very politely, mind you, but shut good and tight.

"Do you mind that I came here?" Finally sensing his confusion, Allene matched it with a little pout of her full, red lips. "I just thought that since I had tickets to that play, we could save time, and—"

"No." Ryan managed a smile. "It's fine, it's just that..." He looked into her melting brown eyes. "I'm really tired, I'm sorry."

"Oh." She looked down at a set of tickets in her hand, and Ryan felt like a jerk. "I...understand."

Ah, hell. "But..."

Allene brightened. "But?" she said with such hope Ryan knew he had to do this.

"But I'll be fine," he said.

"Great! We'll stop by your house so you can shower and change first." She took his hand and tugged him toward her car.

Ryan watched Taylor's building fade away and wondered what Suzanne was thinking. Probably not fond thoughts.

Then he wondered exactly how he should kill his brother. Slowly, he thought. Slowly and painfully.

SEVERAL HOURS LATER Allene dropped Ryan back off at Taylor's building for his truck. Turning off her car, she turned and sent him yet another dazzling smile.

After an evening of those mega-wattage smiles—which Ryan now knew covered up an innate inability to have a conversation that didn't apply to her makeup, her hair or her clothes—Ryan felt a little mega-wattaged out.

He hadn't been able to ditch her. When he'd tried, she blinked wet eyes at him, saying Rafe had promised he'd take her for dessert after, and he'd folded like a cheap suitcase.

Damn it. Now all he wanted was a couple of aspirin and a glimpse of another woman.

Suzanne.

He didn't consider it a good sign that he hadn't been able to get her out of his head the entire evening. It wasn't as if *she'd* wanted to go out with him. Hell, she hardly wanted to talk to him.

But somehow he knew that to be a ruse. That what was happening between them simply terrified her.

He understood that. He felt it himself. But it had to be faced.

Tonight. With that in mind, he turned to Allene with an apologetic smile. "It's late," he said, leaning back a bit when she unhooked her seatbelt and moved in on him. "Allene, wait—"

Nope, she didn't wait, she straddled him, right there in the Miata, which had to be a nearly impossible feat given the gear shift. "Allene—"

"I've wanted to do this since I first saw you there on those steps, all stretched out, hot and sweaty and sexy as hell." Fisting her hands in his hair, she kissed him.

He had a beautiful woman sitting on his lap, trying to shove her tongue down his throat, and he was actually going to fight her off.

What was wrong with this picture?

As gently as he could, he pushed Allene back to the

driver's side of the Miata. She fell there, mouth wet, eyes hot, her body sprawled out and hopeful.

She sighed. "It's another woman, right?"

"I'm so sorry."

She tossed her hair out of her eyes. "It's okay. I knew it."

If she'd known it, he was worse off than he'd thought. Figuring she'd let him off easy, and also feeling a little guilty about it, Ryan practically scrambled out of the Miata. Ran up the steps.

And came face-to-face with Suzanne, who stood there, leaning against the door, arms crossed, face utterly unreadable.

"Hey," he said, skidding to a stop, a little breathless.

Reaching out, she swiped a finger over the corner of his mouth. She lifted it to show him the bright red lipstick Allene had left there.

Then she turned and went into the building.

And this time, the door slammed. Hard.

9

AFTER SLAMMING THE DOOR—why had she done that, she didn't care who Ryan went out with—Suzanne stalked through the dark hallway, up the stairs and straight into Taylor's apartment.

"Taylor?" She let herself in. "I need an ice cream fix!"

"Well, then, come on back! I have a brand new gallon and two clean spoons."

Suzanne stormed into the kitchen, headed for Taylor's freezer and grabbed the gallon container. Since Taylor had sold her antique dining room set to start work on the loft, there was nowhere to sit, so they each hopped up on the counter.

Doing her best not to remember what had happened the last time she'd sat on a counter, Suzanne took the spoon Taylor handed her and dug in.

Taylor waited until they'd each had five good-sized bites. "So." Swinging her feet, she sucked a drop of ice cream off her spoon. "What did he do?"

"He who?"

"He who. Ryan who."

Suzanne studied a swirl of chocolate. "What makes you think *he* did anything?"

"Because he's got a penis, hon. He can't help but be an idiot."

"Yeah." Suzanne sighed. "But for some reason, I always forget that idiot part."

"Well, I have to admit, Ryan does seem to have evolved slightly further than the average knuckle-dragger. I mean he looks at you, *really* looks at you. If you gave him any encouragement at all, I think he'd go for it."

Suzanne snorted and shoveled in more ice cream.

Taylor lifted a brow. "Are you saying he's already gone for it?"

"No."

"Oh," Taylor said with disappointment.

"*I* went for it." At Taylor's shocked laugh, she sighed. "Remember when the electricity went out the other evening? We nearly..."

Taylor put down her spoon. "Nearly *what?*"

Suzanne dug back into the container with more force than was required. "Let's just say the electricity came on just in time and my sanity returned."

"*Wow.* So you nearly..." Taylor sighed. "He's got the *best* body."

"One he took out a date tonight with a woman who looks like a Barbie doll."

"Hmm."

"He kissed her."

"*No.*"

"Oh yeah."

Taylor put her spoon down. "Should we kill him?"

"I'm serious."

"So am I." Taylor hopped off the counter, and looked deep into Suzanne's eyes. "Are you sure you're not mistaken? I've seen him watch you. There is no one else, there couldn't be."

"There was tonight."

"Talk to him."

Suzanne hopped down, too, but kept a hold of the tub of ice cream. She wasn't letting go of her comfort food. "No way."

"I think you should."

"And I think we need to renew our vow to remain single, since you've apparently forgotten it. I'm borrowing this ice cream." She went out the door.

Taylor sighed. "I'll renew *my* vow," she said to the swinging door. "But I have the feeling you won't be needing yours for long."

CONCENTRATING ON shoveling ice cream into her mouth at a rate that would ensure obesity by her next birthday, Suzanne headed toward her own apartment.

Her throat was tight, her eyes burned and it bugged the hell out of her. Good Lord, one would think she actually *cared* who that Neanderthal dated, when everyone knew he dated anything in a damn skirt.

It didn't matter, not one little bit, because she was never going to date again. She was never even going to look at another man again, no matter if he was Adonis.

She'd have to get a vibrator, of course. Or turn lesbian.

No, a vibrator would do.

Reaching out blindly for the front door of her own apartment, she nearly swallowed both her tongue and the spoon on it when she encountered a hard chest instead.

She knew that hard chest.

"Suzanne."

Oh, God, she knew that voice too, mostly because it made her mouth go dry and her thighs clench together.

Two large hands settled on her shoulders. One gentle shake had her raising her head to meet his dark, dark gaze. "We have to talk," he said.

She swallowed her latest bite of chocolate ice cream and thought about that. "No."

"There are things you need to know."

"N-period-O-period, *no*."

"The date was set up by Rafe."

"You poor, poor baby. I bet it was rough."

"Hey, you're the one who said I should go."

Yes. Yes, she had.

"Look, I've come to terms with this..." He waved a hand between them. "This *thing* between us, and you should, too."

"This *thing*? We have a *thing*?" She gaped, then laughed. "Don't be silly, we don't have a thing."

"We sure as hell do." His forehead was furrowed as he opened her apartment door, one hand still on her arm as if he thought maybe she'd bolt. Or slam the door on him.

She considered both.

"All I'm saying..." He ushered her inside. "Is that we might as well see it through."

"Why? To get it out of our system? We tried that!" Exhaustion made her shoulders sag. "Go home, Ryan."

"You don't understand."

"Oh, I understand perfectly. You date obsessively. You're addicted to women!"

"Suzanne—"

"And given what's almost happened between us, *twice* now, I think you're also addicted to...*sex*." She whispered the last word, horribly embarrassed that her mouth seemed to have run away with her good sense. In fact, forget him leaving, *she'd* leave.

He caught her in the kitchen. When he turned her back to face him, he was smiling, damn him.

"Suzanne." He bit his lower lip, and she had a bad feeling it was to keep from laughing. She wondered how he'd look wearing a spoonful of ice cream, and gripped her spoon and gallon tight.

"If I'm addicted to anything," he said. "It's you. And don't take this wrong..." He backed her into a corner. "But I'm not leaving until we have this out."

Bullies had never scared her. Without stopping to think—a problem she'd been addled with since childhood—she lifted her spoon, fully loaded with ice cream, and used it like a slingshot, flinging chocolate ice cream.

It hit him square on the forehead.

He lifted a hand to the spot, then looked at his chocolate-covered finger with shock. A drop of the stuff plopped from his forehead to his nose, and he shook his head, baffled. "I can't believe you did that."

"Believe it." She loaded her spoon again, hit him on the jaw this time. "And there's more where that came from."

"I take it you're not going to be logical about this." Putting a hand on the tile's edge on either side of her, effectively blocking her in, he bent slightly so that they were eye to eye. A drop of the chocolate ice cream fell from his jaw and hit her on the shoulder.

He looked down at it with gleaming eyes before he bent and licked it off.

At the feel of his tongue on her skin, her breath caught in her throat. Whatever she'd been about to say or do—and damn it, it had been good, too—flew right out the window.

"Now." He lifted sleepy, sexy eyes. "Let's try this again." He shifted his big, warm body close without a care for the ice cream dripping over the both of them. "Yes, we need to see this through. I realize you're thrilled as hell at the thought, but—" He grabbed for her wrist when she might have flung more ice cream. "Why don't you let me tell you a few things to see if we can ease your mind." Almost idly, he set the gallon container on the counter, then took her other wrist as well, leaving her pretty much his captive. "First, I do not date obsessively." Dipping his head again, he took another nibble of ice cream off her shoulder and made a low purring sound in his throat before speaking again. "That would be far too tiring."

It was very difficult to follow this conversation with his hands and mouth on her. "But Rafe said—"

"Rafe was wrong. Tonight was a fluke, he set me up when I wasn't listening."

Suzanne blinked at his flat voice. "He said you go out every night."

"Three nights a week."

She saw that his jaw had gone tight, and that the humor had left his eyes. Obviously he was more than a little tense, but what had made him so? *She* was the one picturing him going out three nights a week with a different woman each time. "Fine," she said slowly, feeling more than a little confused. "But you should know, I still consider three dates a week pretty sick."

He stared at her for a heartbeat, then pulled her hands behind her back, holding them there with one of his. This left his right hand free, which he took on a cruise over her shoulder, smearing the ice cream into her skin. "Do you consider three dates a week sick because it's me?"

It had become difficult to concentrate on anything but those fingers. "Uh..."

"Do you?" His fingers traced her collarbone. "Suzanne?"

What had he asked?

"I'm thinking you don't want me dating anyone." More fingers on her skin. "Except, maybe, you."

"Ha!" She meant to sound strong and carefree, but it came out weak and breathy because his finger trailed over her throat with a light touch before he dipped it into the gallon container on the counter.

With a mischievous light in his eyes, he brought that ice-cream covered finger back to her throat and skimmed it to the wild pulse at the base of her neck.

Her nipples hardened.

"I'm leaving the house three nights a week, yes," he said, tracing her collarbone now. "But not for dates." Very lightly he stroked that finger straight down to the top button of her sundress, which was right between her breasts. "And as for being addicted to sex..." Now his fingers played with that first button, and before she could draw a breath, it fell open. "Before I met you I would have said of course not."

"And now?" Good Lord, was that her voice, all light and fluttery and...inviting?

"Well, if we're talking about you and me...then it's quite possible." Another button popped open, then another, and then the strap of her sundress slid off her shoulder. With a little nudge from Ryan's mouth, her breast was free. He studied the white cotton of her bra, then stroked the covered nipple with his thumb, watching it pucker all the tighter with a fascination that made Suzanne clench her thighs tight. "Have I answered all your questions?"

She blinked him into focus and tried to remember. "If you're not dating the entire female species, where are you three nights a week?"

"I'm..." He let out a long breath. "What the hell. I'm going to college at night."

"But... That doesn't make any sense."

"Why? Because I trim trees?"

"What you do is more than that," she said slowly at the unfurling anger in his voice. "You know it's more than that."

"Yes. It's been a way for my family to stay together. It's put food on the table and a roof over our heads. It's been a lifesaver, but it's not the job of my heart, and I need that. I need the job of my heart, Suzanne. I'm getting my landscape architectural degree this year, after six long years of taking classes whenever I could."

He was staring at her with such drive, such intensity. Contrasting sharply was the ice cream dripping off his nose.

"I'm sorry I smeared ice cream on you," she whispered.

"Sorry enough to lick it off?"

Um...undoubtedly. But there was the little matter of keeping her head, so that afterwards they could walk away from each other. "Licking you," she said, "would be very nice, I'm sure."

"Nice?" He let out a choked laugh. "*Nice.*"

"That's not an insult."

"Really."

"Look, I'll admit I feel...a little hot and itchy when I'm near you. But—"

"I really hate that word but."

"But..." She had to smile at his groan. "But...I just have to be careful that we both know where we stand."

"Since you're so determined to keep reminding us, how can we forget?"

"Yeah." His chest just barely brushed against her achy nipples. She bit her tongue to hold her moan in. "You going out on any more dates? Not that I care—"

His smile was slow and devastating. "You care. So do you want to know where we went, or what we did?"

"Neither. I don't care."

"Really? You didn't care at all? Not one little bit?"

"No. Yes. *Yes*, okay?" *And I want to know if you touched her like you've touched me.* He better not have, came her next thought, quickly followed by dismay at the possessive feelings she didn't want. She lifted a shoulder. "What you did tonight is your own concern."

With a surprisingly gentle touch, he smoothed a wayward tendril of hair behind her ear. "I can tell you we didn't smear ice cream on each other's bodies."

"Neither have we."

"Ah, but the night is early." Eyes once again filled with that hot, challenging, oh-so-sexy glow, he slid his hands—still sticky—into her hair.

"You've just put ice cream in my hair."

"Yes." His mouth hovered near hers. "I'm planning on putting it everywhere."

"I don't think so."

"You started this." His lips curved ever so slightly, his expression full of a laughing dare. "I think you wanted this."

"I wanted to…"

"Yes?" he coaxed when she didn't finish. "You wanted to…what?"

Okay, she'd wanted to cover his body in ice cream and eat it off. But that had been when she'd been mad and full of all that wild energy. That had been before, when she'd felt the irrational urge to compete with his Barbie doll date.

But now she didn't want to compete with anyone. "This is *such* a bad idea," she whispered, just as he stroked her jaw and lowered his forehead to hers.

"Probably."

"So let's just walk away," she said desperately.

"I'd rather fight for it."

Panic filled her at the thought, true and heart-stopping panic, because she instinctively knew, she wouldn't be able to resist. "No."

"You're scared. I know. *I know,* Suzanne."

"I'm not scared."

"I'm not like them. I'm not like the other men you've let in your life. I'm willing to fight for this, not just walk away when it gets tough."

Is that what had happened to her? Had no one, including herself, ever fought hard enough to make it work?

"I'm going to fight," he warned her. "Fight for you."

"Very bad idea." Her voice shook, because she knew he'd fought for his family, his life. And he'd fight for her. Oh, God.

He put his mouth to hers, and with nothing more than a light, gentle, soulful touch of their lips, her entire body came alive. So did her heart.

"No," she whispered, putting her hands on his wrists to pull him away, but somehow she ended up just holding on. "I don't want you to fight for this."

"Why not?"

"Because you have a will of steel. I know you do, after all you've been through."

"This is a different kind of fight altogether."

It was, and she knew it. This was a fight of the heart and soul. One she was in no way ready or able to resist. Slowly she shook her head. Reached behind her. Grabbed the ice cream and clutched it to her chest. "You should go."

"I want you, Suzanne. I want to hold you, touch you. Bury myself in you. I want to be with you, see you smile, laugh. Live."

"That's fighting dirty," she whispered, voice thick. "But I can fight dirty, too." Reaching out, she grabbed a very cold fistful of the now slightly melted ice cream, pulled up his shirt and slapped the ice cream low on his belly, just above his jeans. And though she went a bit wobbly at the feel of his warm, hard stomach, she locked her knees together and lifted her chin to nosebleed height.

He sucked in a harsh breath and his jeans gaped, allowing the ice cream to slide down, down, down and out of view. A strangled sound escaped him.

She clapped her hand to her mouth.

Eyes hot, he politely took the spoon from her. Dipped it into the ice cream.

And smiled the smile of the very devil.

"Ryan." She laughed and backed up. Right into the counter. *"Ryan."*

"Yes, that would be my name."

"I don't—"

"Yes?" he cocked his head. "You don't...what?"

"Well..." She smiled a bit nervously. "I don't think

there's any cause to act like children here—" The words ended with an abrupt gasp as he let the ice cream fall off the spoon and down her half unbuttoned, half off her shoulders dress.

Still smiling, he then put his hand over the center of her chest, fingers spread wide, and pressed, smashing it into her skin.

Shocked by the cold, she panted. "Okay, maybe an ice-cream fight is a bad idea."

"I'll agree. So here's a different kind of fight for you." Hauling her against him, ice-creamed chest to ice-creamed chest, he let out a slow smile that started her heart pumping. "Fight back if you dare," he whispered before putting his mouth to hers.

10

"REMEMBER. This...is...just sex," Suzanne panted when they both broke free from the kiss for air. Her chest rose and fell as if she'd been running uphill for an hour, the pulse beat wildly at the base of her neck. "Just sex," she said again. "Right?"

Ryan could feel her vulnerability as his own. "You want me to be honest?"

Her eyes clouded. Clearly she wasn't sure if she wanted honesty or not, and in the face of her confusion, he felt the most overwhelming, most unexpected tenderness.

"Maybe we shouldn't talk," she said.

Disappointment tasted like the bitter chocolate ice cream on his bottom lip. "You want me to go?"

"Yes."

Good. Because while his body throbbed, his mind actually agreed. He took a large step back.

"You're...walking away."

"Walking away," he agreed.

"Good."

"Great."

He had no idea who made the first move, they simply, suddenly, lunged at each other. Ripped at clothing. Sank fingers into hair. Kissed so deeply he had no idea where her mouth ended and his began. "Ryan, my God..." Her voice was ragged and filled with hunger.

"I know. We have to—"

"Yes."

He lifted her up, set her on the counter and stepped between her thighs in one motion, then groaned when she arched to him, sliding against his erection so that his eyes crossed.

"Here?" She practically mewled it. "Now?"

"Here. Now." He tugged the bodice of her dress down, catching it on her arms, pinning them to her side. Oh yeah, that worked for him. Opening her bra, spilling her breasts free, his knees nearly buckled at the sight of them, full and creamy, with rose nipples budded tight, begging for his attention.

"Ryan, free my arms. I want..."

But he wanted, too, and taking advantage, he lifted the spoon and dribbled the soft melting ice cream over her bared breasts.

She sucked in a hard breath, and the chocolate-covered curves jiggled for him, making his mouth water. He had to unhook her ankles from behind his back to work her panties down, but then was able to dribble more ice cream over her quivering belly. Her inner thighs.

"Ryan..." She jerked when a drop hit at the vee of those thighs. "That's...going to be...sticky."

He liked that she could barely talk, that she was out of breath already. "Not if I lick it off first."

Her eyes went huge. "You're going to—"

"Watch." Bending, he put his hands on the tops of her legs, spread them even wider, groaning at the view *that* presented. "God, you're beautiful." And she was, all hot and wet for him, dotted with chocolate topping he couldn't wait to eat off.

She gasped when he lowered his head. *"Wait."*

He lifted his gaze. "Problem?"

"It's just that...I...no one's ever..." Closing her eyes, her cheeks went bright red.

"No one's ever put his mouth on you before?"

Eyes still closed, she shook her head.

He felt a flash of anger at the other men in her life, which was quickly replaced by a surge of satisfaction. He'd be the one to show her what it should be like. "Open your eyes, Suzanne."

When she did, he slid his hands up her thighs until his thumbs met.

She let out a helpless little hum.

With the pad of his finger he smeared the chocolate right over the center of her. "Now."

"N-now?"

"Now I'm going to lick you, just as I promised."

"Oh. Well..."

He licked her.

"*Oh!*"

"Mmm. Chocolate-covered woman." He licked his lips. "My favorite flavor."

"Ryan, I—" The words turned into a little whimper when he licked her again. He liked the rough, needy sound she let out so much he just kept at it.

"*Ohmigod. Ohmigod.*"

When he switched to a nibble, then sucked her into his mouth, she nearly bucked right off the counter. He simply slid his hands beneath her, cupping her delectable butt in his hands and held on. Licking. Sucking. More licking. In a minute, she was on the edge. Then her every muscle tightened, trembled, and he waited for her explosion.

Instead, she tried to close her thighs. "Stop!"

Damn, the magic word. He lifted his head. Her arms were still pinned at her sides, her fists clenched, her every panting breath making her bared breasts shimmer and shake.

Then he looked into her wild, glazed eyes. Her wild, *stressed out* eyes. "Ryan...I'm going to..."

"Come?" he asked gently. "You're going to come?"

Her hair flew into her face when she let out a jerky nod, and his heart constricted with such affection he could hardly breath. "But that's good." He stroked a finger right over the plump, turgid flesh he'd just been sucking on. "Really good."

Her entire body twitched upward, seeking more of that touch. "But—"

"I want you to." Lowering his head so that his breath brushed against her hot, hot body, he whispered, "Come in my mouth, Suzanne."

And with the next stroke of his tongue, she did exactly that with thrilling abandon.

WHEN SUZANNE could open her eyes, she stared at Ryan, shocked. She'd come. In his mouth. *She'd come in his mouth.*

"Good?" he asked with a smile that might have been smug if it hadn't been filled with so much tight need.

She opened her arms, and straightening, he stepped right into them, but she needed more, too. She tugged at his shirt, sucking in a breath when he pulled it over his head and tossed it aside.

He was beautiful. *Beautiful.* She already knew that, but seeing him up close and personal, touching him, gliding her fingers over his hot, hard flesh...

"Tell me you have a condom," she said in a low

voice she didn't even recognize as her own. She'd never in her life made the first move, but she was shameless now, and he'd made her that way.

"I have a condom."

Shocking herself, she undid the button of his pants. Reached for the zipper. The rasp of metal on metal seemed loud in the room where the only other sound was their ragged breathing.

And Suzanne's breathing was very ragged, more so when she slipped her hand inside, past the melted ice cream and wrapped her fingers around him. He was fully erect, needing release, and she was so desperate for the same thing she could hardly contain herself.

"Your bed," he said.

But she shook her head. She didn't want to wait that long. "Here."

He fascinated her, he had from that very first day when he'd dropped out of that tree, but this, right here right now, was taking that fascination to another level and she knew it. He was real, much more real than anyone else she'd let in her life. He had hopes and dreams. He was physical, astonishingly graceful. Powerful.

And aroused. For her.

She wanted him, wanted him in a way that went

beyond the physical, and she was going to have to face that. Later.

His fingers were shaking as he put on the condom. Watching him was the most erotic thing she'd ever seen.

"Ryan?"

His gaze, hot and heavy, lifted to hers.

"Hurry." She slipped her arms around his neck at the same time he caught her up and hauled her to him. With her wrapped around him, he turned from the counter and faced the table. One swipe of his hand sent her mail and a couple of books to the floor before he sat her on it. He was strong and hard, and she'd never wanted anyone as she wanted him. He took her face in his hands, and when they kissed this time it was no simple, gentle touch but a deep, wet, hot statement of raw hunger.

They were both lost in it. He bunched the material of her skirt up past her waist. She used her toes to shove down his pants. He pulled a breast into his mouth, teasing the chocolate-covered nipple with his tongue while she guided him to where she needed him most.

Then he thrust into her, making them both cry out. Using the table for leverage, he pulled back and thrust again, this time going higher, deeper. And then again.

Looking at him, holding his dark, dark gaze, she

burst right out of herself, yet another orgasm, with shocking ease, when such a thing had never come easy for her, never. Always, she'd had to strain and strain, and often had just settled without.

Not now, though she had the sinking feeling it wasn't the time or the place, but the man.

Oh, yeah, it was the man.

He kissed her again, and touched her face. Drew her hands to his chest and moaned his encouragement when they lowered. And she felt, unbelievably, another tightening within her body. Struggling to keep her eyes open, she watched as he drove her higher, then higher still, and at the end, threw his head back, her name on his lips.

Just watching him, so untamed, so uninhibited, hearing him say her name in that ragged voice, triggered her third—her *third!*—orgasm of the night.

But even as the lights exploded inside her head and her body shuddered with the insane pleasure of it all, her mind rebelled. And held back.

Because this was nothing but a single episode. An end to a means. A temporary diversion.

And no matter what her heart cried as Ryan gently put his mouth to hers, no matter what she really yearned for, she wouldn't let herself sink into him.

She'd keep her heart out of it.

FOR RYAN, he came back to earth in slow increments. "If that was just sex," he said, too weak to lift his face away from Suzanne's neck or open his eyes. "I'll eat my shorts."

This was greeted with silence.

Forcing himself, he pulled away from the soft skin of her neck and looked at her.

She, however, hopped down from the table and bustled around, gathering clothes, tossing his to him.

"Suzanne?"

She turned away, staring out the window, into the dark, dark night.

"Hey. You okay?"

She hugged herself, and when he put his hands on her shoulders, she stepped forward, and away from him. "Of course I'm fine. Perfectly fine."

He had a good idea what was going through her head. She was very busy distancing herself, convincing herself that everything was still the same. But she was wrong, nothing was the same, and it wouldn't be ever again. "What just happened wasn't the norm for me, I want you to know that." He'd been with other women, he'd even done it in a kitchen before, once with whipped cream, but even that hadn't been close to what he'd just shared with Suzanne. Chocolate ice cream or not, this hadn't been just sex. When she'd been in his arms, he'd felt...whole. And when he'd sank into her body, she'd shattered him, heart and soul.

"It's late," she said. "I'm sorry." And she walked out of the kitchen. A moment later he heard her bedroom door shut.

Leaving him standing there in the kitchen with his ego on the floor at his feet next to his pants.

TWO MORNINGS LATER Suzanne stood in the same kitchen in which she'd allow Ryan to eat her up, literally. Chocolate was involved this time as well, though not quite in the same mind-blowing manner.

She was putting little dollops of frosting on top of cookies, preparing a dessert tray for her third catering event of the week. A luncheon, a referral from the party she'd catered at Ryan's.

Ryan.

Only two nights before he'd rocked her world right here in this very kitchen, looking at her with those dark, dark eyes as if she could quite possibly be the one for him.

And she'd ruined that by walking away.

Which had left her lying in bed, staring at the ceiling for two nights running, wondering which exact gene she'd inherited that had made her such an fool.

With a sigh, she popped another fattening cookie into her mouth. It made for an even dozen. The chocolate melted in her mouth, the cookie dissolved beautifully.

Well, good. If she couldn't keep her personal life on track, at least she made a hell of a cookie.

AFTER THE LUNCHEON, Suzanne drove through South Village, trying to clear her head. Everything had gone smooth. Better than smooth. She'd booked two more jobs for the following week.

Pretty good for a hobby, she supposed, and ignored the little voice that said it should be more than a hobby.

Maybe she just hadn't been born to be regimented, responsible or serious.

It was afternoon and the streets were humming with action. Businesswomen were out on break shopping and lunching. Men were watching the women shopping and lunching. There were bikers, walkers, joggers...all talking, laughing or, in the case of a roller-blading teen, singing at the top of his lungs. Scents from the sidewalk cafés contrasted with the scents of Southern California air— flowers and smog.

Suzanne stopped to buy a newspaper, thinking she still needed a job, then drove around some more, checking out a few newer cafés and restaurants.

She came back to reality when she ended up at Ryan's office.

To get out or not, that was the question now. She wondered what it meant that she couldn't come up with an excuse for being there other than the simple one. She wanted to see him.

"Hey."

At the husky voice in her ear, she jumped. Ryan stood next to her car, looking so good her hands itched to touch, though his smile seemed a bit strained and there were things in his eyes that...oh, God, the things in his eyes.

"Hey," she said back. "I...just wanted to..." She couldn't remember. "Um..."

He looked at the newspaper on the passenger seat. "Job hunting?"

"Still."

"What's up with the catering?"

"It's just—"

"A hobby," he said with her, then smiled.

"It is."

"I know it. What I don't know is what you're so afraid of." He said this softly, without any censure or reproach.

And maybe that was why she was able to give him a helpless smile and admit the truth. "It's the usual."

"Failure?"

She nodded, struck dumb by how well he understood her. Had anyone ever understood her so well?

"Suzanne, don't you love catering?"

"Of course."

"Don't you love being in charge of your work-day?"

She sighed. "Yes."

"Are you making money at it?"

She nodded, then covered her eyes. "I know, I know, it'd be a perfect way to get responsible."

"I meant it's a good way to make you happy."

No one had ever worried about her happiness, no one.

"Suzanne, just because your past relationships haven't worked out, doesn't mean you'd fail at this."

When she would have looked away, he leaned in and touched her face. Made her look at him. "And since we're listening to what I think...I think I am very glad those other relationships didn't work out. That was fate. You running your own business is fate. And Suzanne? We're fate, too."

She closed her eyes. "Ryan."

"Come to dinner with me."

Bad idea. "I'm not hungry."

"Then let's go walking."

"I'm..."

"Anything, Suzanne." His voice was low, his eyes fierce. "Let's do anything, even just stand here and stare at each other."

That wouldn't work either. She'd made a promise to herself, and no matter what he did to her insides, she had to keep that promise. It was all she had. "I've got to go. I'm sorry," she whispered, and reversed out of the lot, praying she didn't run over his foot.

She made it back home before she let herself think. She needed ice cream. Nope, she couldn't even count on that as comfort food any more because she couldn't eat it without thinking of wild, hot, on-the-table sex with Ryan.

Chips, she decided as she climbed the stairs. She could go for a big bag of barbecue chips. Yeah, that would work, there was absolutely nothing sexy about a bag of chips.

Unless of course they were scattered across the magnificent body of one Ryan Alondo. Now *that* would be sexy because she could start at his toes and eat her way up his long, lean form and—

Bad Suzanne, very bad.

She'd have to skip the chips, too.

Taylor's front door was open. She'd been out shopping at estate sales again, Suzanne thought with a fond grin as she skipped her place and stepped into Taylor's living room. A three-foot-high brass frog greeted her, as did an ornately carved wooden umbrella holder and a glass shelving unit upon which sat a collection of pewter figurines from Alice In Wonderland.

She knew Taylor couldn't help herself, that collecting was firmly entrenched in her blood, but to gather more stuff when she'd only have to sell them off to finish the building? Suzanne wondered how long before they were both out in the street.

There were voices in the kitchen, several low and male, and at least one female, but it was the gathering of men that made Suzanne's heart start pumping.

Ryan? Had he beat her here for some reason? "Taylor?"

"Come on in!"

Suzanne did with pitiful eagerness. There were two men at the table, bent over a set of plans. There was also a young woman, her dark hair cut spikey and close to her face, with a multitude of earrings up one ear. She wore frayed jeans, a handkerchief for a top and sported a diamond in her belly button. She sat filling out something on a clipboard. "Hey."

Taylor sauntered across the small room toward Suzanne as only Taylor could. "What's up?"

Suzanne lifted a brow. "You're the one with a kitchen full of people."

"Oh, well. It's a busy morning." She lowered her voice. "Those two at the table are presenting a bid to renovate the building. They took one look at me and decided they could bend me over a barrel with the price. Of course I've cheerfully informed them they were sorely mistaken. They're now groveling and figuring out how to lower their price like good little boys."

Only Taylor. "And the interesting looking woman?"

"That's Nicole Mann."

At the sound of her name, the woman with the clipboard looked up. She had the most unusual gray eyes Suzanne had ever seen. Taylor jerked her head, indicating Nicole should follow her and Suzanne out into the hallway.

"Suzanne," Taylor said when they were all in the hallway. "This is Nicole Mann. She's applying for a place here. I'm thinking the loft will be ready by next week. Unless you want it back."

"No, I'm set where I'm at." Suzanne smiled at Nicole, who didn't quite smile back. "The loft is great. Nice view of the city now that the trees are gone."

"I don't have the time to breathe much less appreciate a good view." Nicole handed the clipboard to Taylor.

"All filled out?" Taylor skimmed the form. "You're a doctor?"

"Surgeon."

Suzanne was stunned. There was no way this woman who looked younger than she herself could be a surgeon. But Taylor continued talking before Suzanne could ask Nicole any questions.

"And it's just you, right? No roommate or significant other?"

Nicole shuddered. "God, no."

Taylor laughed.

Nicole didn't. "Why is that funny?"

"Let's just say Suzanne and I are on the same wavelength as you, that's all. We've taken a vow of singlehood, just to save us gray hair."

"Works for me," muttered Nicole, but this time when she smiled, it reached her eyes. "Call me at the hospital when the place is ready. It's where I'm at pretty much 24-7."

"Will do." Taylor watched Nicole vanish down the stairs. "You know, there's just something about her…"

"Do you think she has other stuff pierced?" Suzanne wondered.

"Ouch. I hope not. But I meant the feeling I had when I first looked at her. It was the same feeling I had when I first looked at you."

"Yeah?" Suzanne smiled. "Like 'get this girl off my property before her and her bad karma bring a tree down on my building'?"

Taylor laughed. "No. Like she's going to become someone special to me." She nudged Suzanne's shoulder with her own. "Just as you've become."

Suzanne smiled a little, startled by the sudden lump in her throat. "You're special to me, too."

"Special enough to tell me what's wrong?"

"Nothing's wrong."

"Which, of course, is why you've got circles beneath your eyes and you're avoiding talking about you know who."

Suzanne managed a laugh. "I'm not avoiding talking about him."

"Really? Then why won't you say *his* name?" When Suzanne didn't say anything, Taylor said it. "Ryan. Ryan. *Ryan*. Come on, you can say it. Ry—"

"Look…" Suzanne blew out a long breath but had to laugh at Taylor's knowing expression. "Can we talk about something else? Anything else?"

"Sure." Taylor smiled. "How's your catering business going?"

"It's just a—"

"Hobby," Taylor said with her, then shook her head. "Look, hon, I already love you. But you've got a serious case of denial going all the way around. You've got a great business practically running itself, and the prospect of some really good sex. Why can't you just enjoy it? What's the worst thing that could happen if you let yourself be happy?"

She could fail. And…well, she could fail.

And, oh yeah, she could fail.

11

RYAN FOUND HIMSELF inundated with jobs, which coincided with his midterms. Which coincided with his inability to think of anything and anyone but Suzanne.

It wasn't good. He needed concentration. His latest job required him to take down a series of ten palm trees, each a towering seventy-five feet. Big job. Important job. It had been waiting for him for weeks.

So why he drove the wrong truck, with the wrong ladder system and lost two hours of work was beyond him.

The next day he ran out of gas halfway to the job and had to call Russ for a ride, losing another hour of work.

On the third day he didn't remember to pick up Angel from school when she'd called and asked. He'd forgotten his own damn sister.

On the fourth day he miraculously made it to his jobsite without interruption, and felt quite proud of that fact.

But then was immediately surrounded by his two

brothers and sister, all of whom were looking at him so gravely his heart stopped. "What's the matter?" He pictured a serious illness, a death, something mind-bendingly awful enough to put that doom-and-gloom look on their faces.

"You," Angel said gently, then shoved him into one of the folding beach chairs they kept on the job for lunch break. "You're the matter. Ryan Alondo...." She waved a hand. "Welcome to your intervention."

"My *what?*"

"You heard me. Just sit there and listen."

"Yeah." Rafe took off his sunglasses, appearing haggard and worried, and took a deep breath. "Okay, here it goes. First, you're forgetful. You've never been forgetful before, Ryan."

"It's like you've gone blond or something," Russ said, shutting his mouth when Angel glared at him.

"So, you tell us." She stood over Ryan with her hands on her hips. "What's the matter? Are you sick?"

"No. *No!*" he added more vehemently when he saw how worried they really were. "I'm not."

"Are we having money trouble?" Russ asked, because it was Ryan that handled the bulk of their pay, investing it for them.

"Yeah, like, did you take up gambling, and lose everything, and don't know how to tell us?" Rafe asked. "Because if you did, that's okay. We can make more. We just want to know."

Ryan would have laughed if there was anything funny about the fact that he'd really freaked them out. They were staring at him as *he* had stared at *them* over the years—an expression of sober grimness mixed with a lot of love.

The irony was not lost on him. "I didn't lose all our money."

"Is the business going under?" Angel asked. "Because that doesn't matter either, you know that, right? We'll find something else, we'll work at Taco Bell, we'll—"

"The business is good," Ryan said, his voice a little thick because damn, they'd given him a sucker punch to the gut with this reminder of how much he wasn't alone. "Look, I'm sorry if I've been a little out of it lately, but—"

"A little?" Rafe shook his head. "I told you I didn't get home until three in the morning, and what did you say? *Nothing*."

"You got home at three in the morning?" Ryan frowned. "Where the hell were you until then?"

"See? You never even heard me."

"I'm hearing you now. Where were you—"

"Look, kick his ass later, okay?" Angel knelt in

front of Ryan and took his hands. "Tell us what's wrong."

Ryan stared at the three people in the world who meant everything to him, and spoke the utter truth, the truth he'd only just been able to admit. "I've...fallen for a woman."

They all stared at him for a heartbeat, then burst into laughter.

"That's a good one," Angel said, swiping a tear of mirth off her cheek. "You've fallen for a woman. *A* woman. Uh-huh, right."

"As if one would ever be enough." Rafe was still grinning, too. "When we all know you need a minimum of three a week."

"See, now that's not exactly true." But it had been his own deception that made them believe it. "I'm not dating women every night. I'm...going to college. I'm almost finished my landscape architect degree."

Russ narrowed his eyes. "But you *are* dating. You dated Allene just last week."

"I did go out with Allene, but only because Rafe set it up and I didn't pay attention enough to say no. I'm not kidding you, I'm taking classes three nights a week and between that and work and Suzanne, it's killing me. I'm sorry I didn't tell you, I...just wanted to do this for me."

Angel stared at him, then wound her arms around

his neck. "Oh, Ryan. College! We're college buddies! I feel so proud of you!"

"Landscape architecture?" Rafe repeated slowly, then grinned. "How cool is that?"

"But what about the business?" Russ asked.

"The tree business will be here as long as you guys want it."

"So..." Rafe scratched his head. "You've been doing all of it? Just for us? Bro, you didn't have to do that."

"Of course I did."

"I don't want to make this a chick-flick or anything," Rafe said a little thickly. "But that's pretty damn cool of you."

"Landscape architecture," Rafe said slowly. "Yeah. Sounds cool. But...you're not dating the entire female population? Really?"

"Really." Ryan gave Angel, still in his arms, a squeeze. "Sorry."

She pulled free to narrow her gaze on him. "So who's Suzanne?"

"The one." He swallowed and faced the cold, hard truth. "She's the one."

"She's— Oh my God." She put a hand to her mouth while her gaze never left his. "You're serious."

"I'm serious."

Russ groaned and sank theatrically into a chair. "He's fallen and can't get up."

"So what are you going to do about her?" Angel wanted to know.

"Well...I'm going to convince her she feels the same way."

"Why do you have to convince her?" his sister demanded. "Why doesn't she already love you? What's the matter with her?"

"Nothing." Ryan grinned. "She just isn't quite as sure of me as you are."

SUZANNE FOUND a part-time chef position at a restaurant across town. After being her own boss for weeks, she had to admit...working for someone else wasn't as much fun as she remembered.

South Village was fun to live in, and fun to cook in, but this restaurant was upscale. Which meant she was cooking for people who knew what they wanted and weren't afraid to say so. Very quickly she got tired of the same menu every night, and not being able to deviate for fear of insulting a patron.

One morning about a week after what she thought of as "the ice cream" incident with Ryan, she tripped over a package outside her door. Frowning, she picked up the plainly wrapped, odd-shaped box with the pretty silver bow. It was nearly two feet long, several inches wide, and gave off no other clue as to what it was.

She glanced left and right down the hallway of the second floor landing, but there was no one there, so she pulled off the ribbon, then the paper.

And found herself holding a set of beautiful teakwood cooking utensils.

A card fell out, and she scooped it up, her heart accelerating at the words.

Suzanne,

For your catering. I know, I know, it's just a hobby. But maybe you'll think of me when you use them, as I'm thinking of you.

Ryan.

Ryan, the man who'd made her smile and yearn and burn. Ryan, the man who haunted her dreams every night.

Ryan, the man who could single-handedly destroy her in a way no one else ever could.

The gift wasn't some empty-handed gesture, as flowers might have been. The utensils had been bought with her in mind, which meant the gift came from his heart.

That alone made her throat tight, because she couldn't remember ever receiving a gift like this before.

Lord, she must be tired. She hadn't slept well in days. Ryan's fault, as she'd been dreaming about him. If she wasn't dreaming about him, she was thinking about him.

Again, his fault. He'd called, he'd stopped by, and much as she wanted to remain indifferent, she couldn't. Not when every time they easily talked, easily laughed...and easily could have taken it further.

She'd say it was all physical, but that was a lie. It was far more than physical now, and she knew it.

Which made it no less terrifying. She'd failed in her determination to keep him out of her heart. Utterly failed.

That evening when she got home, there was yet another package. Small this time, with another silver bow.

She opened the thing like a kid at Christmas, then right there in the hallway had to sit down.

It was a pewter pin in the shape of a chef's hat, lying on velvet. Etched on the hat was her name. The detailing was beautiful, the pin was beautiful.

And so was the gesture.

This time her fingers shook when she opened the card, and just seeing his words—the ones he'd written in his own hand—made his voice come alive in her head. Her body reacted as if he'd touched her.

Suzanne,

I'm so proud of you. Be proud, too.

Ryan.

That night, wearing the pin on her pajamas and holding the teak utensils in her hand, she sat on her bed and picked up the phone. Dialed. Listened to Ryan say hello in that low, sexy voice. And panicked.

Why had she called?

To tell him to stop buying her presents, that's why. To tell him to stop making her think of him. To tell him this had to stop because she was losing her mind.

"Hello?" Ryan said again.

She bit her lip. Tell him. *Tell him!*

"Suzanne?"

Oh God.

His voice deepened, became intimately familiar. "Suzanne, is that you?"

She closed her eyes. "How did you know?"

"I'd recognize your panicked breathing anywhere."

Terrific.

"I'm glad you called," he said quietly. "I've been thinking of you."

"I...have to go."

"Suzanne—"

"Bye," she whispered in a choked voice and hung up.

It wasn't possible to be more pathetic, really it wasn't. And then, as if he could still hear her, or worse, *see* her, she lay down and put her pillow over her head.

12

THE NEXT MORNING Suzanne woke and ran to her front door. Hauling it open, she looked down at her feet, and let out a helpless little hum of pleasure.

Ryan had come. She unwrapped a set of votive candles, vanilla scented. Her favorite, which he knew, and she melted all over again.

This time the card read:

Suzanne,
   I couldn't find chocolate ice cream scented candles...

Ryan

She laughed.
Then she cried.
She stood there holding the teak utensils and candles, with her pin on her pajamas, staring out into space. What would happen if she gave in?

No. No giving in. Had she forgotten what she did to men? Good men went bad because of her.

Damn, this wasn't funny. This wasn't something

she could walk away from. Suddenly furious at herself for getting in too deep, she headed down the hall.

Suzanne found Taylor in one of the dusty, bottom floor storefronts, looking as put together as always in tan slacks and a pristine white blouse.

"Hey there," Her friend said, not turning around. "I'm getting this unit ready. We need someone with lots of bucks to come in and open a shop or something. I was thinking— Uh-oh." She'd finally turned and took in Suzanne's rattled appearance. "What's the matter?"

"Do you know where Ryan's current job is?"

"Um…" Taylor smoothed her perfectly glossed lips together. "If I say yes, are you going to storm off in your pajamas, holding what looks like salad tongs and a set of candles?"

Suzanne looked down at her sweat bottoms and tank top. Women wore less than this every day. So her hair was undoubtedly rioted and she had no makeup on, so what? She wasn't here to win a beauty contest. "I am, yes. He's…he's sending me gifts, Taylor."

"The bastard."

"I know!"

Taylor stuck her tongue in her cheek. "So what did he send?"

"Not generic flowers. No, nothing as simple as

that. He sent *good* stuff. Stuff I want but would never go buy for myself."

"Really," Taylor said with a tsk and a serious face. "The nerve."

"It gets worse."

"Do tell."

"Well...I think he likes me for more than just the sex."

"Again, what a bastard."

Suddenly Suzanne laughed. Just as she'd always laughed in the face of such emotion. It felt good.

"Oh, honey. Give it up. Marry him."

Suzanne's amusement faded. She stared at Taylor, utterly confused, and miserable in it. "You're as crazy as he is."

"Really? What else is he doing to you besides the gifts and great sex?"

"He won't get out of my head, that's what!"

Taylor grinned. "He's at the Pasadena Target store, taming a humungous set of palm trees."

The store wasn't far at all. She could march over there and tell him this was not funny, that he had to knock it off, and still be back in half an hour. "Thank you," she said, and shocked them both when she hugged Taylor.

Taylor squeezed her back. "What's this for?"

"For laughing at me. I needed that."

She was halfway to the door when Taylor called out. "You going to give him hell, or a big, fat, juicy kiss?"

"Hell," said Suzanne, a thought straight from her head.

But her heart cried out for the big, fat, juicy kiss.

HELD UP BY safety gear, Ryan carefully balanced himself about sixty feet above ground, one foot braced on the roof of the building, the other on his rig ladder. Time to tackle a palm tree.

While he contemplated his next move, something from the corner of his eye caught his attention. A figure striding directly toward Russ on the ground.

A wildly curved, wildly red-haired figure. Her arms were full, her posture animated.

And even at sixty feet, he could feel the fury.

"You've got company," Rafe noted from his high perch.

As if Ryan hadn't already *felt* her. As if his entire body hadn't leapt to hopeful attention. "I see her."

They started down. Suzanne's gaze landed on him and never wavered.

He wondered if that was good or bad.

Bad, he decided, when he caught a glint of the emotion in her eyes.

When his feet touched the ground, she stalked toward him, balancing the things in her arms to free up a hand so she could poke him in the chest with her finger. *"You."*

"Me," he agreed, rubbing his chest. *Ouch.* "It's, uh, good to see you." She was wearing hip-hugging sweats and a little tank top, showing off the body that made him want to beg. God, he missed her. "How are you?"

"I would be just fine, thanks, except you've been leaving me gifts."

"Yes."

"You bought me cooking utensils."

Blatantly eavesdropping, Rafe took off his hard hat and sidled up closer.

"I did buy you utensils," Ryan agreed. "For your business."

"Why?"

Ryan glanced at Russ, who was also apparently unconcerned about eavesdropping, as he'd moved in to hear, too.

"Ryan?" Suzanne's arms were crossed, her foot tapping the asphalt as she not-so-patiently waited.

"Why did I buy you cooking utensils?" Ryan scratched his head and tried to figure out if that was a trick question.

"Yes, why did you buy me cooking utensils? It's a straight-forward question, Ryan."

Oh, she looked magnificent, and furious.

And confused.

It was the last that broke Ryan's heart. "Because they were beautiful and reminded me of you. Suzanne, you cook." He lifted a hand. "It made sense to me."

"Oh, man, you bought her *cooking utensils?*" Rafe shook his head. "Should have stuck with flowers, bro. Chicks like flowers."

Ignoring that, Suzanne thrust out a votive candle. "What about these?"

"You bought those, too?" Russ winced and sent Ryan a pitying look. "Ah, jeez. It's like watching my idol fall right in front of me."

Shooting his brothers dirty looks was a huge waste of time. Ryan did it anyway, but they didn't budge. Fine. He'd kill them later. Facing Suzanne, he said, "I bought those because the scent reminded me of you."

"Oh, dude..." Rafe groaned. "You're going down."

"They...reminded you of me?" Suzanne stared down at the offending candles, then clutched them to her chest as if they were a dozen roses. "Really?"

Ryan nodded, a little confused himself now. Was he still in trouble? Or was he back in her good graces? His head was spinning.

"He meant to buy you flowers and make you dinner and *light* those candles," Russ said, stepping forward. "He just gets all mixed up sometimes. It's his age."

"I didn't get it mixed up," Ryan said, hoping to God he was right. He had no clue, and Suzanne standing there in her little itty-bitty tank top and belly-baring sweats, with her hair wild and free, her face void of makeup, looking for all the world like she just stepped out of bed, gave him no clue.

All he knew was that he wanted to move close and touch her. So he did.

"He's just been so swamped becoming a landscape architect," Rafe said just as Ryan lifted a hand. "Or he would have been more romantic."

With Ryan's fingers on her face, Suzanne turned her lips into his palm. Kissed him. "It *was* romantic," she whispered.

Ryan's heart leapt into his throat. She got it. She really got it. She understood. She thought the gesture of buying her such personal gifts was romantic.

Thank God.

"The gifts were purchased just for me," she said to Russ and Rafe.

Oh yeah, she got it. "Yes," Ryan said. "Just for you." There was no one else. There would never be anyone else.

"They're wonderful," she said to him now. "Wonderful and thoughtful, and...and they made me feel special."

Ryan was pretty much glowing. From the sexual energy, no doubt. From her words and the meaning behind them, too.

And rational or not, hope surged within him.

He just might get lucky tonight. He could almost taste her now. And with his arms around her he could convince her how good they were together....

"What I want to know is," she continued softly, staring right at him. "Why?"

And that was when Ryan got a few important life lessons. First, buying a girl a present was not a direct pass to her bed.

And second, he had no clue what did constitute that pass.

But he could see her mistrust and fear clear enough, and because of that he managed to realize something else. Matters of the heart, specifically hers, couldn't be handled with a few little tokens.

Nope, if he wanted her love—which he definitely did—he'd have to earn it.

The hard way. "I bought you those things to make you feel good. To make you smile."

"Not to soften me up so I'd..." She lowered her voice so only he could hear. "So I'd sleep with you again?"

Ah, hell. Nope. No way would he admit to that temporary crack in good judgment. "Just to make you smile," he repeated, and was rewarded with exactly that.

So when she started to walk away, her hips swinging in such a way that drew his eyes, it took him a moment to assimilate she was leaving. "Hey!"

She just kept walking.

What the hell? "Suzanne?" He drew all sorts of snickers from his crew when he went running after her. Catching up to her at her car, he spun her around.

She was still smiling, so prettily just for him, that he couldn't help but smile back. "You came to just smile at me and leave?"

"No. I came to get mad at you, but I don't feel mad anymore."

"Let's have lunch."

"It's too early."

"Breakfast then."

"I'm not hungry."

"Suzanne." He let out a little laugh. "You're driving me crazy here."

"I know." She pressed her fingers to her temple. "Me, too. I'm sorry. I'm a little confused, Ryan. I just need to think."

"Can't you think with me around?"

"Frankly, no." She touched his jaw. "I don't want to hurt you."

"Then don't."

"I just...need to be alone to think, okay? Good-bye, Ryan."

He snagged her hips and held her still, feeling unreasonably panicked, though he forced a smile. "I don't like that word, good-bye, not when it applies to you and me."

"It's the only one I have at the moment."

Be patient, he ordered himself as she drove away. She cared, she cared deeply, he could see it in her eyes, feel it in her touch. *Just be patient*.

He might as well have asked himself to stop breathing.

13

THE PARTY Suzanne was to cater that night was for a wedding anniversary. Another referral from the party she'd done for Ryan's brothers.

It crossed her mind that it was likely Ryan could be there, but as the party was a fiftieth wedding anniversary, and the happy couple was well into their seventies, she figured she was safe.

That *he* was safe. Because she had no doubt, she would destroy him.

But he probably wouldn't be there, so she could relax. There'd be no long, direct stares that made her knees wobble. No light touches that caused her thighs to quiver. No secret smiles to both lighten and freakout her heart.

"I followed my nose all the way in here," Taylor said as she walked into the kitchen, sniffing appreciatively. "We thought we'd help you carry your stuff down."

"We?"

Taylor turned aside just as Nicole appeared in the doorway.

"I was signing the rental agreement for the loft," she said with a shrug that caused her myriad of earrings to tinkle like wind chimes. "The scent drew us in here." She wore military green cargo pants that hugged her slim hips and a camouflage T-shirt with the sleeves ripped off, emphasizing a tiny, lean and incredibly toned frame. Her short, sleek hair was carefully tucked behind her ears as she leaned over the trays and inhaled dramatically. "My God, you're a genius, too."

"Too?" Suzanne looked at Taylor.

"Yeah, she graduated college at thirteen. Disgusting, huh?"

"I'd give it all up to be able to cook like this." Nicole took another hopeful whiff. "No, I take that back. I don't want to be able to cook like this, I just want to live above someone who does."

Taylor laughed. "You managed that feat, Super Girl."

"Yeah, well, I'll feed each of you whatever you want if you help me load all these trays." Suzanne wondered if she needed to change her blouse, or if anyone would notice the small chocolate stain beneath her right breast. No time to worry about it, she decided.

Nicole looked at her watch.

"What, you got a hot date?" Taylor asked her.

"Work," Nicole answered.

"Food should always take precedence over work."

"You're right." Nicole picked up a tray.

It took four trips down the stairs, and by the time they'd finished, Suzanne was huffing and puffing. "For how much I lug around every day, I should be thin. I deserve to be thin."

"Nah." Taylor jerked her head toward Nicole. "If you were thin like Nicole, for example, you wouldn't have boobs."

With a frown, Nicole looked down at her small breasts.

Suzanne laughed. "I'd give up the extra ten pounds each in a heartbeat."

"Really? Wonder if Ryan would say the same..." Taylor then ducked past Nicole to avoid Suzanne's extended foot. "By the way, I hope he's there tonight, you look great."

Suzanne did not feel great, she felt...harried. She was wearing her usual uniform of a white shirt—with the small chocolate stain—and black skirt, which, upon reflection, actually was kind enough to hide her biggest flaw—her hips. "It doesn't matter to me one way or the other if he's there."

Taylor snorted. "Right."

"Singlehood," Suzanne said. "Remember?"

"Hey, *I'm* keeping the vow," Taylor said. "Don't you worry about me."

"Or me," Nicole muttered, sliding the last tray in the back of Suzanne's car and swiping her palms on her thighs.

"You're too cute and young for such a vow," Suzanne said.

Nicole lifted a brow. "I'm twenty-seven. Same as you I'd guess. And besides, a woman can never be too young to decide no man is a good man."

Only a few weeks ago, Suzanne would have said amen to that. But the image of Ryan came to her—tall, dark and...well, hers.

Damn him. "I've got to go."

"Give Ryan a kiss for me."

"Shut up."

Taylor smiled knowingly at Nicole. "She's going to give him a kiss for me."

Suzanne sighed. "There are containers in my fridge. Help yourselves to dinner."

Taylor and Nicole high-fived each other and vanished up the stairs.

Suzanne got into her car, and all the way to the job lectured herself on the reasons why singlehood was a good idea. Why she'd made the vow in the first place.

And all the way there, the reasons didn't make much sense.

An hour later the party was in full swing. She was in the kitchen, racing around, humming to herself, when she turned toward the door and froze. Ryan stood in the doorway looking at her with an expression that completely stole her breath.

And suddenly, she couldn't remember a single one of those reasons she'd recited to herself on the way over here. She couldn't remember anything but how he made her feel.

He wasn't wearing his usual jeans and work shirt, but instead a pair of khakis and a collarless thin sweater that clung to his broad shoulders and chest in a way that made thinking all but impossible.

Before she could recover, his long, long legs swallowed the distance between them. "Hey," he said softly.

How was it possible to be so off balance just by looking at him? He hadn't even touched her, couldn't touch her when he had his hands in his pockets as he did, and yet her heart had already taken off.

He slipped his hands out of his pockets to tuck a wayward strand of her cursed hair behind her ear. Just a gentle touch, an easy touch, one he drew out by not retracting his hand right away, instead letting his finger trail down her cheek.

"I have work to do," she managed.

"Okay." He ran his finger over the pin on her

blouse, just above her breast. Her nipples would have hardened, but they'd already done that at the first sight of him.

She lifted a tray but he took it out of her hands.

"Ryan—"

"Let me help."

Before she could say that wasn't a good idea—if she let him help, she would feel obligated to him, and if she felt obligated to him, she might do something stupid at the end of the night like beg him to make love to her—he simply leaned close and kissed her cheek. Just her cheek, just a quick connection, and yet her entire body reacted. Wanted more. No other man had ever had that kind of power over her.

And, she realized, no man ever would. Her legs wobbled at this realization.

Ryan walked out the double swinging doors of the kitchen with the tray, leaving her standing there... stunned. Aching.

"Fine, then. Take the tray." Muttering beneath her breath about beautiful, bossy men who had to have their own way, she whirled back to the counter and began to fuss over another tray that had gotten a little sideways on the drive.

"Why is it that every cook I know mutters to themselves?" asked a female voice.

Angel. Suzanne didn't turn around immediately,

as she wasn't ready to face yet another Alondo. "How many cooks do you know?" she asked lightly.

"Well, there's you. And my brother. Even though we tease him, Ryan is pretty handy in the kitchen, did you know that?"

No. No, she didn't. She didn't know a lot about him, and despite the pull low in her belly at the thought of him, say standing barefoot in his kitchen whipping them up a midnight snack, she decided that was a good thing.

"He cooked dinner for us every night after our parents died." Angel looked over the dessert tray carefully as she spoke. "Through homework. Through basketball games. Through me being a stupid, vain and mean teenage girl. Through Rafe and Russ not wanting to sit down for family dinners without Mom and Dad. Through thick and thin, Ryan was there, making us dinner." Angel plucked up a brownie. Popped it into her mouth. Chewed, then closed her eyes and moaned with pleasure. "Oh my God, this is sinful." Her eyes opened again. "He always made a veggie." She shuddered. "Usually a green one. He made us eat it. I used to hate him for that."

Suzanne pictured the three of them, Russ, Rafe and Angel, young and scared and hurting, being gathered together for dinner by Ryan. Ryan, who just wanted to keep his family together and safe. Ryan, who'd do anything, including giving up college, simply to make that happen.

A man like that was different from any man she'd ever known. A man like that wouldn't just walk away when the going got tough. A man like that would say only what he meant, and would never, ever, hurt her on purpose.

She couldn't ruin a man like that...right? So what was she afraid of? What was she really afraid of here?

Maybe, she thought with a hitch in her breath, nothing. Absolutely nothing.

Worse, maybe the truth was she'd hidden behind her fear of nothing.

And that made her a coward. "And now?" Suzanne asked quietly. "How do you feel about him now, knowing all he sacrificed to keep you guys together?"

"I love him more than anything or anyone," Angel said simply. She popped another brownie. "Mmm." She licked her lips. "And I'd seriously hurt anyone who hurt him."

Suzanne leaned back against the counter and considered the younger woman. "Is that some kind of a warning?"

Angel looked at her. "Do you plan on hurting him?"

"Don't be silly," Suzanne said with a little laugh

that didn't hold any real humor. "I don't have the power to hurt him."

"Is that what you really believe?" Clearly disappointed with Suzanne's response, Angel put her third brownie back. "Really?"

Suzanne pictured how Ryan had looked a moment ago, eyes hot and aching.

For her.

In their wildest dreams, neither of them had ever intended for this...this *thing* to go as far as it had. She knew that, just as she knew what they'd wanted had little to do with it. Their hearts had taken over.

Oh, Ryan. What a pair we are.

As if he could hear her thoughts, he came back into the kitchen, looking bigger than life. Dividing an even glance between his sister and Suzanne, he raised a brow. "What's the matter?"

"Nothing." Angel went to him and kissed his cheek.

"What was that for?" he asked.

"Actually," Angel said. "It was nothing at all." And with a long look at Suzanne, she left.

Suzanne busied her hands with another tray. "She's a good person," she said, not looking at him. "That's because of you."

"You haven't seen her at the crack of dawn on a

school day," he murmured, coming close. "Don't give me credit where it's not due."

"Ryan—"

He put his fingers to her lips. "Hear that?"

When she spoke his fingers brushed her mouth. "All I hear is the music."

"Exactly." It had gone soft, dreamy and slow. Taking the oven mitt out of her hands, he drew her close.

There was nothing in her but need so she went against him, then pressed closer still. They rocked together a little, for the longest time, just being.

When the second song came on, he shifted closer still, and so did she. His hands molded her body.

She returned the favor. She couldn't help it, the feel of his big body against hers drew out every emotion she had, and apparently there were quite a few more than she'd imagined.

He had one hand low on her spine, the other, entwined with hers, lay against their thighs. Gently gliding his jaw to hers as they swayed together right there in the middle of the kitchen, he sighed.

And so did her heart.

The music seemed to flow through her, through them, until she couldn't tell where she ended and he began. He was passionate, earthy and, she suspected, rather demanding with those he brought into his heart.

Knowing that only made hers beat faster.

And yet the physical contact wasn't enough. She wanted to tell him some of what she was feeling, only those feelings were so jumbled up and confused, she didn't think she could put words together to justify them.

She had actions though, and didn't actions speak louder than words? She lifted her face to his, wanting that connection, the deep, soul-searching kiss only he could give her.

He gave it, and at his sound of pleasure, she melted into him. It was the most erotic thing she'd ever done, body to body, mouth to mouth, fully dressed, imagining them otherwise. She'd never felt so hot in her life.

Then, as all good things do, it ended. The music died away.

And Suzanne pulled back. "I'd...better get busy."

He ran his thumb over her lips, the ones he'd just been sucking on. "This catering...it's working out for you."

"Oh. Well." She backed up, turned to the sink. "It's doing okay. For a hobby."

"Am I just a hobby, too?"

"Uh..." She turned on the faucet full blast. *Resist, Suzanne.*

But suddenly she didn't want to resist. She wanted

him, and more of the amazing feelings she always had in abundance when she was with him.

She wanted that more than she wanted anything. Whipping around, both a smile and his name on her lips, she faltered.

Because he was gone, leaving her standing there under the harsh glare of the kitchen lights, body aching and burning.

Just as she'd probably done to him over and over.

IT TOOK HER another hour to clean up the job. Ryan never came back.

By the time she'd packed up and got everything in her car, it was late.

Still, she found herself outside Ryan's place with her hand raised to knock.

This was stupid. She had no idea what to say to him. Lowering her hand, she turned away, then swore out loud. Then she whipped around again and knocked before she could change her mind.

Ryan answered the door in low-slung sweats and a pair of wire-rimmed reading glasses hanging by the earpiece out of the corner of his mouth. He had a book in one hand, a pencil in the other, and seemed less than pleased with the distraction.

Until he saw her. "Suzanne?"

She managed a little smile, though in truth she was

so nervous she felt a little sick with it. "Hi." Stepping close, she pulled the glasses from his mouth, put her hands on his bare chest, leaned in and kissed him.

Shock held him immobile for only the barest of beats before he dropped the book and the pencil to put his hands on her hips. But instead of pulling her close, he held her away, so that she couldn't arch her hips to his. "Are...you alone?" she asked.

"Yes."

He was alone, he wasn't pulling her close, and she didn't know what to do. Staring at his amazing body, into his deep, deep eyes, her mind racing frantically, she slid her hands over his chest. She simply couldn't stop herself. Over his hard pecs, his beaded nipples...

"Suzanne...what are you doing?"

She took some comfort in the fact his voice was low and strained. And underneath his sweats, he wasn't able to hide a thing, including the erection she yearned to rub up against. "Ryan..."

He just looked at her. Not coldly, no there was nothing cold in his gaze as it held hers, but neither was he going to help her.

Please don't let me be too late. "I want to make love with you," she whispered, feeling her face heat there in the dark on his porch.

"You mean you want to have sex?"

She'd hurt him, even though she'd looked Angel

right in the eye and said she couldn't. She could, and she had. "Not sex, no."

He didn't look convinced, so she ran her hands down his arms to his hands, which she entwined in hers.

He still held himself rigid.

She simply leaned in closer and put a kiss on the corner of his grim mouth, then slowly made her way over his firm lips to the other corner.

His eyes drifted shut, his thick lashes fanned against his cheeks.

"Please, Ryan." She outlined his lower lip with her tongue, and ripped a deep shudder from his big frame. "Please? Let me love you."

With a rough groan, he hauled her close. *Thank God.* Hauled her up and against his big, hot body, whirled around, stepping over the threshold, kicking the door closed behind them.

"No holding back," he grated out.

She wrapped her arms around his neck, but he held her off another moment, looking into her eyes with a fierce look of intent. "Say it," he demanded.

"N-n-no holding back."

"Promise."

"I promise," she whispered.

She'd barely gotten the words out of her mouth before he'd planted her up against the front door, his big frame holding her there, which freed up his hands to run them boldly up her body, touching every inch of her.

Heaven. Being touched like this by him was heaven on earth. "Ryan, I've been such a fool about this."

"Yeah. But I love you anyway." He held her head in his big hands, holding her still while he ravished her mouth, before lifting a fraction of an inch. "Are we clear on that, at least? I love you, fool."

14

WHEN SUZANNE just stared at him, mouth open, eyes wide, Ryan figured he should be sorry for letting the words slip, but he wasn't. Her cheeks were flushed, her mouth wet from his kisses. The pulse at the base of her neck was frenzied, her breaths were coming in short little pants as she fumbled behind her for the door.

"Let me guess," he said, not especially kindly, as she'd ripped him right open. "You have to go?"

"I..."

Having her this close again stirred him beyond belief. His heart raced in tune to hers, and he spread his fingers over the small of her back. "All I can say is...don't."

"You love me."

"Yeah. I wasn't looking for that to happen, believe me. I thought I had all I needed." He offered a grim smile. "I was wrong, as it turns out. I've never felt this way before." He whispered this, saw her eyes sparkle with unshed tears. Slowly he slid his jaw to hers while his fingers glided up and down her back, very lightly. "I know you think you'll hurt me, but—"

"Ryan—"

"I'm a big boy, Suzanne."

"I know. I know. Ryan..."

When he bent his head, she met him halfway, and it took only an instant for their bodies to remember how good it was between them. Their hands fought for purchase—skin, clothing, it didn't matter. Ryan couldn't touch her enough.

With his mouth on hers, he lifted her up against him, and though he was insane with wanting her, he managed to get them down the hallway to his bedroom.

He'd actually straightened his bed that morning. Setting her down beside it, he tore the blankets and sheets free and turned back to her. "Suzanne—"

She'd crawled on the bed and had come up on her knees, making every thought dance right out of his head. He moved to the edge of the mattress until his knees bumped it. They were face-to-face now, and slowly, so slowly, he reached out to run his hands down her sides, her hips, to her thighs, which he gripped the backs of and pulled out from beneath her.

With a gasp she fell to her back. "Ryan."

"Right here." He followed her down, meeting her waiting mouth with his, sucking in a harsh breath when she danced her tongue to his. He pressed his hips forward to show her what she did to him, and in response, she dug her fingers into his butt, pulling him harder against her.

Oh yeah, he liked that. But they were too...dressed. Surging up, he skimmed off her clothes, flinging them over his shoulder one piece at a time to her breathless laughter. By the time he got to his, she was lying there open and gloriously nude, waiting, her hips arching just a little, which drove him right out of his living mind. Finesse flew out the window as well, so that when his legs got tangled in his sweatpants, he simply tore them off. She let out another laugh that backed up in her throat when he bent to her breast. With a little growl, he sucked hard at a tight nipple, catching it lightly between his teeth, making her clutch at his head, holding him to her as she cried out. Oh yeah, he liked that, too. By the time he repeated the torment on her other side, she was panting his name with every breath.

Gliding his hands down her body, down her gloriously lush body, he watched as he touched her, as her eyes glazed over, as her head thrashed back and forth on his pillow, and thought this is it for me. *She is it for me.*

"Love me," she whispered.

"Always." He skimmed his fingers down her thighs, then back up, between them now, parting her, exploring her tight, damp center. He found what he sought and gently squeezed.

She let out a strangled gasp and thrust against his hand. "Love me," she said again, and reached for him. "Please, Ryan, love me."

"Open your eyes. Watch."

Her cheeks flushed. "I—"

"Watch," he repeated a bit shakily now because he was dying, dying, to sink into her. "No holding back, you promised."

She swallowed hard. "Now, then. Ryan, now."

"After I taste you," he whispered, and put his mouth to her.

With the first stroke of his tongue, she bucked right into his waiting mouth. Perfect. With his second stroke, she let out a sobbing breath and gripped his ears so tight it was possible he'd never hear again.

Who needed to hear, he thought, and stroked her. And then again, until she was thrashing beneath him, requiring him to hold her still to keep his mouth on the mark.

"Ryan...please!"

Obliging, he sucked her hard into his mouth, and she came in wild shudders that nearly triggered his own release right there on the sheets. Getting a condom on was tricky, but he managed, then guided himself to her creamy center.

Her eyes, dazed, held his. "Yes. Now. *Now!*"

His beautiful, passionate, impatient Suzanne. He pushed deeply into her, then deeper still.

"*Please*, Ryan!"

Oh yeah, he would please. He gripped her hands with his, linking them together as he kissed her again, and then again, making love to her mouth as hard and deep and as urgently as he was making love to her body.

This time when he withdrew, then thrust home, there was nothing gentle or slow about it. "Suzanne." He couldn't help but say her name in wonder, and again in awe, as, fingers and mouths and hearts linked, she took him to a place he'd never been before.

When her muscles tightened around him, when she came again, he strained against doing the same. But he couldn't have held back to save his life.

Burying his face in her hair, he didn't even try.

HE AWOKE with the sun on his face. For a moment he hovered in a dreamy state, half-awake, half-asleep.

He wore only an erection and a dopey grin, both a direct result of the memories of last night.

It was his own little miracle that she'd come to him in the first place, and he still didn't know why, but he would. After he woke her up properly, by kissing every inch of her body, of course. It was only fair to return the favor, as last night, after finally falling asleep in each other's arms, he'd awakened with her mouth on him. That wasn't a memory he'd ever forget. He'd fisted his hands in her wild hair, wondering what he'd done to deserve her in his life. Then all wondering had ceased, and so had thought, when she'd swirled her tongue over the tip of him in tune to her stroking hands. He'd thrown back his head and surrendered as she delivered him the orgasm of his life. He'd still been in the throes of aftershocks when she'd climbed up his body and tangled her tongue with his.

He'd been with his share of women, far less than he'd been reputed to have, but still... He knew what was out there, knew what was expected. He knew how to have recreational sex. He knew how to pleasure a woman, and be pleasured in return.

And never, not once, had he lost control. Not the way he had with Suzanne.

With those three little words of love on his lips yet again, he opened his eyes, rolled over and reached for her.

Only he was alone.

Completely alone.

SUZANNE HURRIEDLY stripped down and stepped into her own shower. She had so much to do, but being in the hot water, with the steam rising all around her, caressing her body...it sidetracked her with thoughts of last night.

Soaping up, her touch reminded her of Ryan's touch. She smiled dreamily, her brain whirling on high without her permission. Ryan didn't even have to be in the room to lighten her heart, and she'd never felt anything like it, not with anyone, including three ex-fiancés.

She'd never *allowed* herself to feel anything like it.

Should she take the time to shave? She ran a hand up her leg and shivered with more memories. Ryan had used his fingers, his mouth, his body to keep her sated. She even bore physical proof, a whisker burn on her throat, one on her breast, and yet another on her inner thigh. Then there was the delicious soreness between her thighs.

He loved her. *Loved her*. Ryan Alondo loved her.

She knew he hoped to seduce her into accepting that love. If only he knew. He already had, and not just with his body. He'd seduced her with his wit, his smile, with the way she felt when she was with him.

She wanted to do the same for him. She'd better hurry. She had a lot to do.

THAT AFTERNOON, Angel delivered an envelope to Ryan at his office.

"I already have today's mail," he said, distracted by the stack of bills he had to pay, the bids he had to put together and the fact that his heart had been torn in two.

"It didn't come by mail," Angel said cryptically, and dropping the envelope on his desk, walked out of his office.

"Angel!" He frowned when she didn't come back—when did she ever listen to him?—and opened the plain white envelope wondering what now.

It was an invitation.

Since he'd never had the social life everyone thought he had, he didn't often receive such things. But someone was having a party.

He wondered if Suzanne would cater it. If she'd ever admit to herself and the people in her life that that's what she wanted to do.

Damn, stubborn woman—

He opened the invitation and stopped thinking altogether.

Dear Ryan,

   You are cordially invited to the opening of my catering company, Earthly Delights.

   Tonight, seven o'clock. RSVP isn't necessary.

   Please come,

                                        Suzanne

AT SIX O'CLOCK Ryan walked into his kitchen. Rafe was rifling through the refrigerator. Russ sat at the table in front of a plate of leftovers, having clearly already helped himself.

And then there was Angel, who sat on the counter eating Ryan's last can of Pringles.

"Hey," they all said to him, mouths full.

The mooches. "I thought you all had places to live. Other than here." Ryan went for a glass, filled it with water and downed it. He'd have preferred a beer, but he had a feeling he was going to need all of his wits about him tonight.

At Suzanne's.

She'd be busy, of course, with the opening of the catering company he was surprised she'd even admitted to having.

Far too busy for him.

Rafe still stood in front of the open refrigerator, staring inside. "I'm still starving."

Ryan rolled his eyes, as his brother had been born starving. "You can eat at Suzanne's."

"Suzanne's?"

"The opening." He shoved Rafe aside and shut the refrigerator door. "Surely she invited all of you."

Angel, still on the counter, kicked a dumbfounded Rafe. "Of course she did."

"Well, drive yourselves over there." Ryan knew he had little to no chance in hell of talking his way into Suzanne's bed, but he didn't have too much pride to try.

Rafe stood there blinking slowly. "But—"

Angel kicked him again and smiled brightly at Ryan. "Of course. You go ahead, we'll...uh, catch up with you." Hopping down, she took Ryan's arm and propelled him to the door. "You go ahead now, bye-bye."

Before Ryan could shake her off, she'd shoved him out his own door and shut it.

"Bye-bye to you, too," he muttered, and got into his car.

HE PARKED in front of the building where it all began, where he'd first dropped out of a tree and seen the woman who would change his life.

It seemed like a lifetime ago, not just a month ago.

He'd certainly lived a lifetime since then, and had seen where he'd like his future to go. But apparently wanting something and getting that same something were two different things.

Seeing Suzanne again in a casual atmosphere, especially after last night, was going to rip his heart right out. But she'd clearly come to some important decisions about her life and its direction, and he'd be there. He'd smile and talk, even laugh if it was required. Anything to help her in the evening ahead.

And if in the process he was crippled by anguish and regret, well, it wouldn't be much different from how he felt right now, would it.

The building had slowly started to change to better fit its surroundings. With the trees tamed, and two gone completely, it had a more lived-in look, despite the fact that the two storefronts on the bottom floor were still empty. Empty but not deserted, as the dust and grime had vanished under someone's careful care.

And thanks to Taylor's insurance, the hole in the third floor loft was nearly mended. There was much more to be done, a complete renovation, in fact. He'd helped Taylor narrow down all her contractor bids, and had suggested several reputable engineers. The rest of the antiques she'd been collecting for so many years would fund the project. In no time, she and the building would be on their way to shining prosperity, fit for its South Village address.

Closer now, he could see a sign in the window of the bottom left storefront unit.

Coming Soon!
Earthly Delights
Catering by Suzanne Carter

She'd decided to open a shop as well? He couldn't believe it, and his heart nearly burst for her.

Even as he ached for himself.

Expecting a crowd in her apartment, wondering if she'd purchased any more furniture than the kitchen table he knew so intimately, he went up the stairs.

At his knock came nothing but a rustling, then a low oath.

"Suzanne?"

More rustling, then a harried, "Yes! Come in!"

Stepping inside, he took in the place with one sweeping glance and smiled. Nope, still no furniture, but the living room and its floor-to-ceiling windows sparkled clean and smelled like lemons. On the clean hardwood floors, she'd placed a few throw rugs that added a lived-in touch.

She had a live potted tree by one window, which looked similar to what had crashed through her loft window not too long ago.

At this blatant, obvious laugh-at-life, he grinned.

There were candles everywhere, along the walls, on the wide wooden window sills, all lit, casting a lovely glow on the early evening.

There was also one glaring detail he hadn't failed to notice. Except for him, there were no people. No celebration, no friends, no customers. No one. "Suzanne?"

The swinging kitchen door rattled but didn't open, and he heard another low oath. "You okay?" he called out.

"I'm...nearly ready— *Damn it.*"

Cocking his head, he moved closer. He reached out to open the door, but paused when he heard a soft rain of more oaths.

"Idiot," came her soft scathing voice. "You are such an idiot to think you could pull this off when you're so nervous you can't even light a candle."

Unable to hold back his curiosity, he opened the door. Suzanne was hunched over the table. On a tray was an ice-cream sheet cake, decorated with chocolate writing he couldn't yet read and a mass of small white candles, of which she was attempting, unsuccessfully, to light.

Instead of her usual hostess outfit of a white blouse and black skirt, she wore one of her loose, gauzy sundresses that he so associated with her and loved. Her long tanned, toned limbs, her nervous smile, her wild hair, all of it, every bit of her, made him physically ache.

"I can't light the stupid candles," she said.

"Here." He ran his fingers down her arm to her shaking fingers, and lit them with her. "But if this is an ice-cream cake, you're going to melt it before your guests arrive."

She sucked in a breath and looked up at him. "My guest, my *only* guest, has arrived."

15

HE JUST STARED AT HER. "What?"

Suzanne took a deep breath. She needed a hundred deep breaths. She set down the matches, turned her fingers so she could hold his hand and let out a shaky smile. "You're the only one I invited."

"So..." He looked confused, poor baby. "You're *not* doing this? The whole catering company thing?"

"I'm doing this." She hadn't been prepared for the disappointment in his gaze, and realized he didn't understand. That was her own fault. "I'm serious about the catering, and I'm serious about..."

"You're serious about what, Suzanne?"

"You. Ryan, I'm serious about you."

He looked down at their entwined fingers. "You had a funny way of showing it this morning." He lifted his head and pierced her with those dark, *hurt* eyes. "Why did you sneak out of my bed like that, without a word?"

"I..." She bit her lower lip, searching for the right words. She'd been searching for them all day, a way to put meaning to how she felt. "I woke up first. You were wrapped around me, all warm and fast asleep and..." She blushed. "So incredibly sexy. I couldn't stop looking at you."

"You should have done more than look."

Oh, his eyes were hot, and deeply intense. Her insides stirred. "Yes, I should have. But I didn't want it to be in bed when I tell you for the first time. I didn't want you to wonder if it was the heat of passion or just the moment."

"When you tell me what?" His expression was carefully blank now, as if braced for a blow.

And her heart cracked. "When I tell you I love you." Her throat tightened. "I love you so much, Ryan."

He blinked. Put his hands on her upper arms and lifted her up to her toes so that they were nose to nose. "What?"

She smiled at his hoarse voice, though she was shaking so much she wondered if he'd be able to hold onto her. "Did you know, before you came into my life, I'd never had a man's undivided attention? A man who really believed in me and what I could do? I mean I had men who—"

"Suzanne."

"Wanted me. I had men who—"

"*Suzanne.*"

She swallowed. Bit her lip. And finally, slowly, looked up at him. "Yeah?"

"Say it again."

She put her hands on her face. Kissed him lightly. Sank into him when he wrapped his arms around her. And felt her heart mend itself. "You taught me things about myself," she said. "Did you know that? I learned to be me. That it was good to be me. To follow my hopes and dreams, no matter how impossible it looks, no matter what the chances of failure are. The catering, for example. All I needed was a little encouragement—"

"Suzanne." He put his forehead to hers. "I love you. I'll always love you. And in a minute, I swear, I'll give you all the encouragement you want, *anything* you want, but I really need to hear you say it again."

"Well, I was getting to that." Breaking free, she went for the cake, turned it to face him. "It's starting to melt already."

Ryan sighed. Okay, so she was trying to seduce him with the ice cream. Cute. Hot, even.

But it was a testament to how intensely he felt for her that he didn't feel a sexual stirring but a deeper one, one of the heart and soul. "I don't want cake—"

"Look."

He stared down at the ice-cream cake, at the letters

she'd painstakingly put there, the ones that spelled I Love You.

They were starting to drip but he got the picture.

She loved him.

She put her hands on his chest, wound them up and around his neck. "With all my heart, I love you."

Hearing the words loosened the fist around his heart. Made him light-headed with joy. "I feel as if I've been waiting a lifetime to hear you say that."

"I'm sort of hoping we have a lifetime ahead for me to keep on saying it." Reaching out, she skimmed a finger along the cake. Studied the chocolate ice cream covered finger with a light in her eyes he was beginning to appreciate greatly.

"I was thinking we should probably get married," she said, and on that shocking statement, she stroked his throat with her finger.

He sucked in a harsh breath at the cold. "Married?"

"Yeah." Dipping her head, she licked the ice cream off his throat as if he were a lollipop. "Mmm," she said very wickedly and made him groan.

"I figured since I took so long to figure out how to get what I want from life," she said. "I don't want to waste any more time. I know what I want, Ryan, and that's you." She put her mouth to the corner of his, then looked up at him. "You have a problem with a woman who knows what she wants in life?"

"No. I'm in love with one."

She smiled widely at that, and he returned it, knowing his entire life was right here in his arms. "And it looks like I'm going to marry one."

Epilogue

A WEEK LATER, Suzanne, Taylor and Nicole sat on the loft floor eating ice cream. The gallon had been provided by Nicole this time, as well as the plastic spoons with which they dug into the container.

Good, practical Nicole.

She'd moved in the night before, so Taylor had decided they needed a house-warming party.

Any excuse to consume calories.

"So, you're really going to marry him, huh?" Nicole took another bite and looked at Suzanne with curiosity. "As in forever?"

"Yeah." Suzanne grinned. "I really am."

"Pretty scary stuff."

"I know." But she sighed with pure pleasure at the thought of finally being a bride, not an ounce of resistance left. "It's right this time. This time it's really right." She smiled at Taylor. "I guess I'm breaking the vow."

"That's all right." Taylor didn't look upset. "Nicole and I plan to keep it going."

Nicole nodded solemnly. "Definitely."

"Good luck." Suzanne thought about her own determination and how she'd happily relinquished it. "Because believe me, love can come out of right field and stab you in the heart before you know what hit you."

"We won't need luck," Nicole said with a determined shake of her head. The silver rings up her left earlobe tinkled prettily. "No way, no how. No man is going to weasel his way into my heart."

"I'm with you, Super Girl," Taylor said. "It doesn't take luck to stay single, just common sense."

Suzanne smiled smugly and went for another spoonful of ice cream. Unlike her two new best friends, she knew common sense had nothing, nothing at all to do with matters of the heart.

Be sure to catch Nicole Mann's story,
TANGLING WITH TY,
Temptation 914 coming in February 2003.
*Return to South Village to see what
happens to Nicole's vow of singlehood!*

Turn the page for a sneak preview...

1

TY O'GRADY TURNED from his work at the knock on the door. He'd left it open for the pizza delivery. "I'm back here. Come on in." Hopefully they hadn't forgotten the beer this time, he seemed to be in a mood for it. Standing up, he stared down at the computer one more time. How to deal with this...?

"Ty?"

Not pizza, but Nicole Mann. Her wide, gray eyes stared into his, and in a flash, pure lust sped through his blood.

And between his thighs.

Her mouth opened, then carefully closed. On instinct he looked down at himself and realized he hadn't put on a shirt or fastened his jeans.

"I thought you were the pizza," he said. The metal on metal glide of his zipper as he fastened his jeans seemed extraordinarily loud, echoing between them.

"Uh..." Nicole jerked her head up and stared into his eyes with a blank expression, as if she couldn't remember what she was doing there.

Lord, that was arousing.

As though she remembered, she thrust out a set of blueprints. "From Taylor." She slapped a file against his chest as well. "You've got the job, Mr. Architect." And she turned away.

"Nicole."

She did not turn back to look at him. "Yes?"

What had he been about to say? Something. Anything. Just so she didn't leave. "I...got the job?"

"I just said so, didn't I?"

Ah, his sweet, sweet Nicole. "Well, then. We need to celebrate."

She pivoted to face him. "Celebrate?"

"Mmm-hmm." Oh, yes, he was enjoying that spark of temper and heat in her eyes.

"You didn't look in the mood to celebrate, just now. You looked mad." She put a hand on her hip.

Maybe he had been, but he wasn't about to discuss it with her. Setting down the plans and file, he soaked up the sight of her. She wore hip-hugging black jeans and a plain black tank top that didn't quite meet the jeans. The peek-a-boo hints of bare, smooth skin decorated by a diamond twinkling from her belly button made his mouth water. "What does it matter what mood I was in? I'm in the mood to celebrate now."

"Well, I'm not."

That could be changed. He cocked his head. "If we're both full of temper and restless energy then we might as well pool our resources, darlin'."

Her brows came together. "Let me guess. We could pool our resources in the way of say...having wild animal sex, maybe up against that wall?"

God, she was something all riled up. "Well..."

"You're thinking about it, aren't you?"

"Oh yeah, I am." And it was one hot thought.

She crossed her arms over her chest. "I only agreed to bring you the plans so I could tell you I'm not going to act on my attraction to you."

He felt heat spear him. "You're admitting to an attraction?"

The look on her face was priceless. "Oh, just forget it." Then, she upped the ante by putting her hands on his chest. Staring down at her own fingers, she spread them wide, as if she wanted to touch as much of him as she could.

"What are you doing?" he asked a bit hoarsely.

"Pushing you away." But she wasn't pushing.

He put his hands over hers, entwined their fingers. She let out a slow breath, and he did the same. Then their gazes met.

He leaned forward a very tiny fraction of an inch so

that their mouths were lined up, but not quite touching. She licked her lips. Swallowed hard. Stared at his mouth. She arched her body just a little.

"Just do it," she whispered.

"Do what?" he asked huskily, teasingly.

"Just kiss me!"

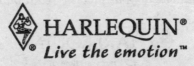

There's something for everyone...

Behind the
Red Doors

From favorite authors

Vicki Lewis Thompson

Stephanie Bond

Leslie Kelly

A fun and sexy collection about the romantic encounters
that take place at The Red Doors lingerie shop.

**Behind the Red Doors—
you'll never guess which one leads to love...**

Look for it in January 2003.

HARLEQUIN®

Makes any time special ®

HARLEQUIN® *Blaze*™

From:	**Erin Thatcher**
To:	**Samantha Tyler;**
	Tess Norton
Subject:	**Men To Do**

Ladies, I'm talking about a hot fling with the type of man no girl in her right mind would settle down with. You know, a man to *do* before we say "I do." What do you think? Couldn't we use an uncomplicated sexfest? Why let men corner the market on fun when we girls have the same urges and needs? I've already picked mine out....

Pasqualie, Washington is about to see some action!

Don't miss three new linked stories by rising star Temptation, Duets and Blaze author Nancy Warren!

HOT OFF THE PRESS
February 2003

A HICKEY FOR HARRIET
A CRADLE FOR CAROLINE
April 2003

Available at your favorite retail outlet.

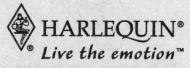

Live the emotion™

Visit us at www.eHarlequin.com

COMING NEXT MONTH

HTCNM0103